A LLULL IN THE COMPASS

The world is running down. People are mysteriously disappearing, leaving behind only small stains of glycerin. Overhead, mysterious objects are appearing just beyond our atmosphere, and deliberately burning themselves to dust as they fall toward earth. Some say our machines are absorbing us, some say aliens have come here to commit suicide.

A small band of wanderers spins the wheels of a Llull Machine, trying to make their way safely through a collapsing world, and trying at the same time to solve the mysteries and save themselves—and an unexpected next generation.

Borgo Press Books by W. C. BAMBERGER

43 Views of Steve Katz

And in Conclusion, I Would also Like to Mention Hydrogen: 11 ½ Essays & 1 ½ Stories

Honesty is Explosive! Music Journalism, by Ben Watson (Editor)

Kzradock the Onion Man and the Spring-Fresh Methuselah, by Louis Levy (Translator and Editor)

A Llull in the Compass: A Science Fiction Novel

Locust Gleanings: Essays, Reviews and Other Interregna on Books, Language and Literature, 1984–2009

William Eastlake: High-Desert Interlocutor

The Work of William Eastlake: An Annotated Bibliography and Guide

A LLULL IN THE COMPASS

A SCIENCE FICTION NOVEL

W. C. BAMBERGER

THE BORGO PRESS

MMXI

A LLULL IN THE COMPASS

FIRST EDITION

Published by Wildside Press LLC

www.wildsidebooks.com

DEDICATION

*For **Aja**, as always,*

and with thanks

*to the memory of **Andre Norton**,*
for life-long inspiration,

*and to **Rob Reginald**,*
for the invitation

CONTENTS

ACKNOWLEDGMENTS

"The Wonderful Widow of Eighteen Springs" was written by John Cage, the lyrics adapted from James Joyce's Finnegans Wake; *the lines beginning "Our dumb city" are from Kenward Elmslie's "Meat," as recorded on his* Palais Bimbo Lounge Show *LP. "Put My Little Shoes Away" is a traditional Appalachian ballad sung in the persona of a dying child. "The World Turned Upside Down" is said to have been played by the British when they surrendered to Washington at Yorktown. All other lyrics are by the author.*

I'm convinced that every constructive idea will appear in many heads at the same time and quite irrationally; one should therefore not speak carelessly about the seemingly confused and crazy; it generally contains the germ of reason. — Paul Scheerbart

Perhaps a little bit of absolute truth on any one question might prove a general solvent, and dissipate the universe. — Samuel Butler

Every answer deepens the mystery. — E. O. Wilson

CHAPTER ONE

MEAN JEAN SPUN THE wheels of the thinking machine. She was leaning a little against the incline of the freeway ramp, oblivious to it, as we walked the rising parabola. Dully tapped the guard rail with his knuckles, Bo high-wire-walked down the dashes of the center line, and I brought up the rear, falling a bit behind the others as I looked out from the concrete and steel heights across the miles of flat farm land gone so colorfully to seed. Sagging fence lines and ditches choked by low brush broke the land into irregular squares like a giant game board. Any time I wasn't turning the wheels myself I gravitated to last in line, surrendered to woolgathering. Mean Jean knew my habits well and called back, "Alastair, keep up!" She no more bothered to look back than I bothered to keep up.

As we walked upslope on the warm concrete expanse, I smiled as I always did when we trudged around any large interchange, feeling its camber tilting us toward its low center. "Every force evolves a form," said Mother Ann Lee, and I agree with her. (Some of the forces that acted upon her were those of abuse and miscarriages, and the form that emerged was the

Shakers, a religious sect that preached Holy Celibacy—so a self-eradicating group. And I wonder: if she were alive today would she suffer a cook-off?) But the fact that the centripetal forces of the highway interchange should summon up the lucky form of the four-leaf clover always struck me as an instance of justice in a joking mood. Few machines in our history made for worse human luck than the city-devouring automobiles. Many ghosts remain of their formerly triumphant selves, all parked. A car on the road is now a rare sight, the driver surely gone a little too far past sense, driving with his or her head out the driver's window with eyes closed. Soon after the cook-offs began, the expressways first swelled with aimless scurrying, then quickly began emptying—after one of those inexplicable global shifts in psychology we all underwent altered how we felt in the driver's seat (a panicky loneliness), population per car rising until riders were pressed against the window, and then seeming to pop like a bubble. Where cars had once flashed in juggling tight formation, their electric engines whining a minimal music, we now straggled in the sun. We were rounding the leaf, on our way home—by what route we couldn't say. Only Llull could say.

The banked concrete was warming us from below, the late afternoon sky was a deep jay-blue, and we would soon be back at the track where I could admire Marcella from a distance. So I was mostly on the happy side, with only the lingering edges of the old buzzwords—"planning," "drive," "direction," those obsolete but deeply-instilled American compass points that were decaying, in me as in all of us, through their stubborn half-lives all too slowly—keeping my happiness from feeling complete. Those points were whispering a little louder than usual that morning, kibitzing; I should be going somewhere, doing something significant rather than keeping to our Llull-prescribed circles. That unhealthy drive was part of the reason I wasn't the designated spinner that day. Mean Jean, comfortable in the part, knew how to concentrate on not thinking— the new, paradoxical strategies for survival often led us along a range that ran from Zen to Zeno and back again—as she spun the layered cardboard and vinyl wheels of the disorienting logic device that led us.

Mean Jean was in charge of the wheels that day because when I awoke, even apart from the compass whisperings, I was feeling decidedly Aristotelian; an unusually clear-sighted outlook, with even morning's first thoughts coming together in dovetail joints, had unexpectedly crept into my mind while I slept. (I think I even dreamt of Zipf's law, from my old field.) Our wandering group had sometimes let ourselves be steered by urban legend, often by superstition (though both tend to have too much of a root in something factual), or by those few things we still found that we could romanticize. Pauli had once read that the Navajo Indians (Are they still down there? Pauli had heard that they'd retreated up to the heights of Black Mesa along with the Hopi, erasing even the few poor washboard roads behind them) were led on each day's hunt by whoever was feeling the most competent. Life being what it is, we stand that principle on its head: Mean Jean, who had yesterday come across in a hidden locker beneath the grandstand a cache of antique bottles—*E & B Beer*—said she felt particularly disoriented this morning, so I felt confident in giving her the wheels and assuming the comfortable role of follower. We had known where we wanted to go that day, to a small strip mall one exit up from our track, but we let the Llull Machine chose our turns, let it inject just the degree of arbitrary choice, of the roundabout that made us feel a little absurd, and so reasonably safe. We had raided the food mart at *Turing Gas & Charges*, but our primary goal had been the small sporting goods outlet next to it. We were tired of all being dressed alike—for the past two months we had been outfitting ourselves from the racetrack's souvenir stall and we were all after a New Fall Look.

Clothes, food, dandruff shampoo, mint tooth-paste, anything we needed or wanted, was plentiful, easy to come by now. The looters and hoarders, mohawked cannibals, slavers and hot-rod assassins in leather dusters we had expected to rise up out of the downfall-of-civilization movies we had all seen had never materialized. Something of suburbanites' ease lingered here in the outlands even after the collapse in the wake of the two mysteries. Our thought was that anyone with a predator's heart had set off for DT or one of the other sinks. Aside from three pink-capped stagehands I'd encountered in the earliest days, we had never met wilders of any kind. It wasn't really a return to prelapsarian days—the confusion and fear were too present, if at a low simmer—but we could move around safely enough. "A post-apocalypse for wimps," Kyle had said. He had carried a fish-gutting knife and seemed deeply disappointed. I had wondered if he would veer off and light out for Sink DT or Sink EDO a few miles south, but that never happened. Maybe if he had lived until he ran out of those little red pills he popped so incessantly....

Llull had taken us to the little mall directly enough, but the route back gave me a mouse-in-a-maze feeling. Still, I followed Mean Jean without a word. She, however, was muttering a blue streak. The Llull machine, with all its deliberate randomness, had over time showed me some profound things about my pack of fellow wanderers. Once we had decided that the non-control of the Llull Machine should pass from one of us to another, turn and turn about, it didn't take long to see how those who seemed the most headstrong among us—Whiteman and Kyle while they were with us, Pauli (who, to be fair, was ADHD)—had the most difficulty, although not with handling the concept of the Machine, or even with the idea of surrendering their will to it. (I never thought Mean Jean would, but she inexplicably turned out to be our most adept operator.) What they found difficult was the freedom to interpret what they saw. As soon as I explained that they could read almost anything they wanted to into Llull's string of words, they would suffer a stage-fright-like lockjaw.

I, for my part, was very comfortable letting the wheels direct us, and with passing along the first thing that came to mind as I read them. In Orwell's vision, a symptom of the implosion of civilization was that words were made to mean their opposites; in the reality of such a collapse it turned out that unhinged words were a source of security. I've always been very much in favor of passive processes. The more that can get done without effort or expenditure of energy on my part, the busier I feel. This is in fact what was behind my decision to become a topologist—a mathematician who studies those elements of any form that remains the same no matter how you twist its shape, even if you turn it inside out. There are always constants that can be followed through every turn, and the mathematics of this following is beautiful. Before the cook-offs, before the sinks, before our night skies began to fill with the beautiful sad streaks of the Lems, Artificial Intelligence had been the tiara of intellectual fashion— flashy and pretentious. But I have always preferred the Natural Intelligence of numbers—every equation is a bit of perfect balance. Being a mathematician is like being an old-time rancher who opens a sluice and watches the water flow downhill in precise courses down to his field; music by Aaron Copland, something loping and wide-open.

I no longer told anyone that I was a topologist. Instead I passed the truth through a mental prism (it was still all there, just separated out into its elements, with some of the angles changed) and said, "I was an actuary." Where in a saner world everyone instinctively ran from anyone in the insurance game, I was at this point considered irrelevant enough to the workings of post-cook-off life that I was accepted with a shrug. So, while I still admired how the running course of numbers eventually ends in a beautiful pool of fact independent of anything I might do, I did so silently. While I strolled along behind Mean Jean, Dully and Bo, watching the packs filled with scavenged food and our fall wardrobes slung over their shoulders swing back and forth as they walked, I silently worked out the ratios of their heights to the points where the swings of their packs were all in sync.

It took half an hour to reach our off ramp, that and half again that long to trek the stretch of access road to the track. High above the gull-wing drive, welded atop the steel-framed sign, an old-school dirt track racecar glinted in the bright sun. It was short and everywhere curved, with flared exhaust ports along its side—a jet-black ocarina high against the sky. We passed through the gates and Dully detoured to slap the sides of one of the decorated school busses—bright pink springs and the nearly-forgotten cartoon character Gerald McBoing-Boing, painted here with a cowboy hat on—as we made our way back to the stands. He was looking forward to our planned blowout.

The Flat Rock figure-8 had been a good stop for us, although here we'd lost Kyle and Whiteman to some mutual madness. Whiteman had been a lawyer; Kyle a drug dealer. But as soon as they met one another, back on the prison grounds, they'd discovered that they had an enormous number of things in common. They had had similar opinions on almost everything (that a drug dealer and a lawyer should be so much alike surprised no one); they had the same tastes in music (gnat note guitar solos obligatory); they were both drawn to the short, fully-packed form of Mean Jean (Whiteman took his loss to Kyle with a laugh and a few consolation reds); they tended to not only finish one another's sentences, but to begin them, as well. But within a few weeks after we had moved to the track they'd begun getting on each other's nerves. Their opinions still matched up to something, by my rough reckoning, above the ninetieth percentile, but they began to hate one another for no reason that anyone else could see. Then one morning, we found them dead, out in the lift area. They appeared to have bashed one another's skulls in with large wrenches, appeared to have done it—sadly, absurdly—simultaneously; beyond the ninetieth percentile to the bitter end.

So we'd lost Whiteman and Kyle, but gained Bo. Not too bad considering the times we'd been through. But we had decided that it was again time to move on.... Had we? In my mind it seemed the idea had come out of nowhere, had decided itself and summarily shanghaied us to carry it through. Ideas have their idiosyncratic little ways, poorly enough understood by their hosts, men. Ideas can lie in wait and surprise you when you least expect it, or appear with a blaze like the sun. We are always at their mercy.

The idea of leaving put us into the typical loop: Staying where there was a cavernous enough space that a band of less than a dozen people could stand to live in it together made good sense, but good sense seemed to be something that carried its carriers over the edge into cook-offs—I had reviewed for everyone the broken-field reasoning that led me to this idea— with no one sure of where that edge might be. So we needed to move along, but then, that made good sense, as well. It sometimes seemed that good sense was inescapable, a devil waiting around every corner to trip us up again. The Llull Machine was meant to act as a restraining order against it.

In the end we decided we also needed to do something on the mindless side as a send-off, something pointless on a scale large enough to counteract any encroaching good sense concealed in our move. Balance is everything. So, because tomorrow we were going to hazard a trip to.... Well, Llull would tell us where tomorrow. Tonight we were going to drive the figure-8. Dully had found a cowboy hat of his own was looking forward to seeing McBoing-Boing go up in flames.

We dropped our packs on the picnic tables Pauli and Todd had set out in the sun. Bo began arranging the silverware in his usual way: forks and knife points jammed into the bread—the loaves bristling like porcupines with sterling silver quills. We had been lucky in Bo finding us. He had made almost no sense at all when we first met him. He had simply appeared one dry day at the Flat Rock figure-8, dripping wet.

"Where am I?"

"You're in Flat Rock," Pauli had answered, looking up from the pizza oven stone he'd reclaimed and was drawing on with a wax crayon.

"I meant what country," Bo said. "Am I in Canada again?"

"Nope."

"Are we at the top of the falls or the bottom?"

Pauli smirked. "No falls around here. '*Flat* Rock?'"

"Flat-lined at Flat Rock," Bo said, and shrugged.

I touched Pauli's arm, between two coils of the Ouroboros tattoo that wound around it, and stepped forward.

"What falls are you talking about?" I asked him. Pauli turned back to his crayons.

"Niagara."

"That's 250 miles east of here."

Bo beamed. "Gravity came through!"

"You've had problems with gravity?"

"With its attitude. It's been avoiding me. I think I offended it." He shrugged again. "I'm Bo. Are you happy?"

"Nice transition," said Mean Jean, standing a few feet away, with her arms crossed and one big beautiful hip shot out. Bo's thought processes clearly had their own unique geometry.

"Am I happy? To tell you the truth," I said, "I don't think about it. Not any more." Marcella and Syd were, I knew, somewhere under the grandstands.

"You?" he asked Mean Jean.

"On a smiles per click basis? I do OK," she said.

"I've never been," Bo said. "So I decided to go over the falls." He shrugged once more. His shoulders were definitely part of his thinking process. "I'm a St. Catharines kid," he said. I knew that was a city near the Canadian side of the falls. "So it seemed the most convenient thing." And he was still a kid, maybe fifteen. This was another stroke of luck, I thought then. Adolescent brains haven't yet formed reliable decision-making centers. "I went to the falls, to the observation platform? I stopped at the junk shop and bought a sack of root beer barrel candies, and swallowed them all, for the sugar rush. Then I got beneath the platform and jumped out as far as I could."

"And yet here you are." It was Marcella. Her feet were bare and we hadn't heard her coming up behind us. She led Syd by the hand.

Bo looked hurt, but Marcella didn't mean anything: she looks at everyone she meets with her telescope turned the wrong-way around, seeing them as being as small as possible. "I think the root beer barrels kept me afloat," Bo said after a moment.

Marcella was scowling, but this was her habitual expression. My guess was that she had been beautiful all her life, and the scowl had first developed as a natural defense against men's gazes, against decades of unsolicited attention, and that the empathy she seemed always to be exhibiting only increased her burdens—and her scowling. She was narrow-hipped and tall, and walked with a slight back-lean and a sway as subtle as the tuck at her waist. There was a ruddiness to her skin that suggest a touch of the Irish. When her rare smiles came her mouth opened evenly, not corners-first as most of us smile—she was either all in or all out; she had very little truck with the middle ground.

Marcella's hair fell almost to her waist. It was a miracle of dusky gold curls, as close-compassed and antic as the spirals of ribbon streamers. She habitually wore it loose and forward, and it covered her temples to the outside corners of her eyes and hid half of the high sweeps of her cheekbones. She was about thirty, but had the angular physicality of a teenager and wore her curls well. She peered out from behind them, coolly gauging what and who she saw, deciding whether she could be bothered with it—and nearly every time, she couldn't. She was immune to obligation. Except, it seemed, to that of shepherding Syd.

Marcella had, in a life before the cook-offs began, been someone who braved the contagions and misanthropic bruisings of venturing into unhinged homes to assess the damages being done to young children. Children like Syd, whom she had somehow saved when the new psychological undertows had swirled her parents off to God knows where—most likely to a sink.

Syd never smiled at Marcella, or at anyone else; she never hugged back when we hugged her. "She was left alone twenty hours a day in a basement rec room by her parents," Marcella said. "They both worked, and each suspected the other of trying to unfairly dump more of the parenting work on them. So unless they were both home to keep an eye on one another, no one ever talked to Syd or even picked her up. If she cried they just turned up the television. Some emotional links never had a chance to grow inside Syd when their time came; now they never will." Still, Syd was a sweet-looking little girl, with beautiful gold skin and snapping black eyes, and we all looked out for her, fed her, picked her up. She found us convenient, I thought.

For a mathematician, I have spent too much of my life thinking about people's motivations, although always at a distance, passively. Sometimes when Marcella bent over to pick up Syd I could see the tattoo splashed across the pebbles of her backbone, but I'd never been able to decipher it in those quick glimpses—Snakes? Wings? Rorschach test? I always looked, and was always of two minds about it: First, I thought, this was the mark of a follower of a fashionable-pain schedule, a crowdling in-the-midst, which was good for our band's unbalance (and unbalance now seemed to be a crucial element of survival). But on a personal level, and for the same reasons, it was disappointing, as well. Because she was so beautiful I had imposed free-thinker traits on her. Funny how even admiration at a distance produces its own little disappointments.

But Bo had quickly made his peace with Marcella's scowl, and she with him at times acting like he needed a surrogate mother. Together they set out the spread on the two metal tables, and we sat down to our last big meal at Flat Rock. All of us—except Syd, who always had to explore the artistic potential of the food she was given—ate quickly.

Then we fired up the school busses.

Through all the wrenching psychological shifts that had descended on us like flows of paint running down the insides of all our skulls simultaneously these past fourteen months some constants had remained. The instinctive, congenital human hatred of school buses was one of these constants.

Todd, who had been a dentist, had restored them all to running order, and we let him choose first: he chose the shortest bus, a smaller target. Mean Jean chose the oldest Bluebird, pulled her helmet on and climbed aboard; Pauli took the seat just behind her. Dully started McBoing-Boing and I was left with a team bus that, even after years without windows, still smelled of socks and jocks. The hammering sounds of diesel engines echoed off the concrete grandstands. The sky was going indigo, and Todd fired up the one generator that still had a cup of fuel in its tank. The pole lights flickered, then burned brightly above us. Todd ran to the short bus, and we slowly moved toward the figure-8.

Marcella had turned up her freckled nose at the opportunity to participate in the bus conflagration and, taking Syd by the hand, she went up to the announcer's booth. From my seat in the black and yellow hornet-striped bus, I could just see the bright wheat of her hair. There was a box of digital music clips that had been abandoned there and she let Syd claw through them and pick one at random. So above the snuffling of the diesel engines, over the nails-in-a-rock-tumbler chatter of the generator, we could hear the bright trebles of a jump blues:

G-String girls and a neon moon
"U-Turn Inn" reads the sign on the door
I'm drinking brew with a pack of fools
El-Train passes and we all roar
T-shirt boys spending midnight pay
Why am I here?

We started slowly, feeling how our busses would take the curves, getting our stomachs used to the way the tall machines swayed, like small boats on deep swells. Driving one behind the other, our four busses took up nearly a quarter of the track's total length. Todd pulled away suddenly, his shorter wheelbase letting him cut the corners harder, and we were off. From my position at the back of the pack I could see into Mean Jean's bus as she took the curve in pursuit of Todd, and could see Pauli bouncing up and down on the seat behind her, laughing. Dully swayed his McBoing- Boing back and forth across the track to keep me from passing, trying to delay me where I would be the first to block the crossover when the leaders came around.

But in a destruction derby no one wants to ram with the front of the vehicle—that only endangers the engine. So my first damage came as Todd took a quick short cut across the infield and hooked my left rear quarter. His bumper went flying and the rear door of my bus crashed open. I checked the mirrors, but couldn't see any more damage. Dully must have seen me looking in the mirror, because he slammed on the brakes and I rammed the rear of his bus. I put a good long fold across its back, but I could see that my hood was sitting crooked now, one side heaving as if it were about to fly into the air.

Mean Jean had slowed, too, and pulled off into the infield. I heard the grate of gears and her bus began backing toward the track, churning up dirt as it came. She spun the wheel to the right and bumped up on the track in time to slam Dully's bus just behind the driver's window. McBoing-Boing tipped onto two wheels and I saw Dully frantically yanking the wheel to the right. The bus settled back on two wheels but was headed off the track into the rocks in front of the grandstand. I could see Marcella in the announcers box, but the busses were so loud that I could only hear the beat of the music she had let Syd select: a polka.

Todd, meanwhile, had come up behind me and pulled up along my right side. With a slight nudge and a burst of acceleration he sent me bouncing off toward Dully. He and I both lost some traction in the loose stones. My bus got a grip first, and leaving my engine to its fate, I rammed Dully full on just above his right rear wheel. I heard a screech and my loose hood flew backward, slamming hard against the corner post just two feet in front of me. I closed my eyes and jerked the wheel, and when I opened my eyes again I was looking at the underside of McBoing-Boing. I had tipped Dully onto his side and was pushing him now as a sound like a jackhammer came from my engine. I stopped and backed away from Dully. I looked for Mean Jean and Todd and they were both back on the track, far enough apart that neither was a danger to the other. I trundled my sweat-smelling yellow heap back onto the track, and went after Todd. Steam was coming out of the engine, and a burning smell. Just then the generators swallowed the last of their fuel and the track went dark except for our headlights. I knew I only had a few minutes before the bus would lurch to a stop, and I left the track entirely, chasing across the infield, trying to intercept Todd's Special Ed bus as he came out of one of the top curves. Todd saw me, and tried to swerve, but Mean Jean, backing down the track toward him, fishtailing and barely under control, rammed him and forced his short bus into the right front quarter of mine, just above the tire. His bus buckled, its frame bent, and I was spun half way around. Mean Jean kept her foot on the pedal, plowing us along the track. Dirt and gravel flew in long roostertails; moldy jerseys, books, pink underwear, and tiny bits of chrome steel flew around the inside of my bus—something nicked my ear and blood was running down my neck, and still Mean Jean plowed on. She shoved us tighter and tighter together until the metal over our tires crumpled and we heard the explosions of blowouts. She ground her gears then and slowly drove away, waving back at us.

I suddenly remembered Dully, jumped to the track and ran toward his overturned bus. He was already out, running toward us. "It's on fire," he was yelling, and we all three started running toward the other end of the track where Mean Jean and Pauli were standing, watching. There was an explosion behind us, but it was a very small, mouse squeak of an explosion, and we turned to see the flame burning in a bright red fringe along the entire length of the bus, like a low flame on a giant gas grill.

I was surprised by how much I enjoyed the sight of the mayhem we had wrought. I had never hated school, and had no particular memories of school bus rides, and I had nearly begged off driving as Marcella had. But now I was glad I had gone along; seeing these three wrecked black and yellow giants made me unexpectedly happy. However much school had given me, it had also taken, and had also been where I, like everyone else, had first encountered distant and disinterested forms of compulsion. In the senseless destruction of those hulking yellow beasts a little bit of the compulsion that rules so much of our lives had been (retroactively) punctured, overturned, and was going up in flames. And that felt good.

But, as is too often the case, my good feeling was marbled with a sad wistfulness. I found myself wishing that all the compulsions that we felt in our lives would come out of hiding, would assume the form of black and yellow lumbering giants. Because then we could recognize them, we could defeat them. As it was our biggest compulsions were invisible to us even as we obeyed them. Then I shrugged that sad and absurd thought away, and just watched the flames devour the busses.

CHAPTER TWO

MEAN JEAN AWARDED HERSELF the first bottle of the warm *E & B*, then passed bottles to each of us as we gathered at our evening fire. We all sat drinking and looking at the skies. There was long moment when only the white scattering of stars showed above us, but then the first Lem came through. This one burned a deep green. Among the many things no one understands about the Lems is why they burn with so many different colors. When the first few appeared, their bright streaks, like colorized meteorites taking over the classic late night black and white theatre, were a welcome distraction from the panic we all felt as the cook-offs continued, as more and more people—with no pattern we could find to the who or where—simply vanished, leaving only a small, wet pool and a quick burst of heat. The disappearances were instantaneous, they were final; many of them were real-life locked room mysteries. Many of those who disappeared first were the dazzlingly brilliant among us: engineers and scientists, mathematicians, astronomers, various selections from across the entire Asperger's Syndrome spectrum. That I was still walking around made me feel both relieved and obscurely insulted: had I always thought too much of myself? But then, maybe I was the obsidian or black glass type, my glintings not as showy.

My own first-hand encounter with the cook-offs was a little more spectacular than most—in fact it joined the ranks of video sensations for a time. I was doing grunt mathematics for a quantum negentrope, a specialist in restoring order to devolving systems. Etheridge, the negentrope, had started trying to explain some quantum calculus to me while he absent-mindedly calibrated the new pulse-and-receptor system that would allow the equipment's self-repair gleaners to step up to the latest algorithm. He was one of those people who did mathematics and nothing else his every waking moment. We were standing near the wall of a surveillence firm's war room as he brushed in his final calibrations, as smooth-fingered as a sculptor, and he simply vanished. One minute he was attempting to explain to me how, "Even when $dy/dx = 0/0$, dy/dx *doesn't* $= 0$ because the differential relation still exists *as a relation*," and the next minute he didn't exist. Before my breathing stopped, I inhaled the ozone smell that always accompanies cook-offs, felt the heat, like a sunlamp being turned on for a quick burst and then off again. Humans are supposed to have a wired-in fight-or-flight response to terror situations, but my reflexes have always favored a third option: a cold fast needling everywhere, coupled with the inability to move or even think. I thawed slowly, as slowly as those around me stood up from their chairs. One woman was already whimpering, one man crying silently and looking up at the ceiling, his fists opening and closing as his hands shook. I looked down and saw "the stain." An oily-looking damp spot, never more than a yard across, a stain that analyzes out as a residue of glycerin.

This wasn't the first cook-off, of course, not even the first in our state, and had this been all there was to it, the incident would have simply been a five-minute blip on the screens and then gone rather than becoming legendary. But then the NHS investigator arrived, a tired-looking woman who said the NHS people were all trying to find some logic in all the cook-offs. No one had been able to find any pattern, except the obvious— the way the cook-offs seemed to have started on one side of the world and then spread around, which told us nothing we could use. She said she had the specifics on a number of incidents stored in her palm deputy and was working on it full time. Her face was Liberty Bell shaped, and her bulldog jaws were set with determination. I went through what had happened, and she asked me to stay close in case she had any follow-up questions. The staff kept their distance from the stain—and from me. The investigator thumbed through a series of screens on her deputy, snapped it closed, and held it out toward me.

"Come here and hold this for me," she said. "And when I ask for it back, I mean I want it back *now!* You understand?"

She then took something else out of her bag. It was a simple GPS. I watched as she checked the GPS screen again and again as she also ran some coordinates. I saw her eyes narrowing, saw her mouth scribbling shapes, without actually speaking aloud. She stared at her GPS and said, "I have...an idea," her voice sounding as if it were echoing through a drain pipe. "I might not know what *caused*.... I need a compass. *Now*."

"Why do you need a compass when you have a GPS?"

She looked as if she were about to laugh and then she vanished too, leaving behind a second glistening stain. You couldn't have asked for more drama—it wouldn't have fit, would have burst the reality. But it was real: at least three people must have had photo nets somewhere on their persons, because for days afterward you could access images of me, standing boneless as a scarecrow, shivering speechless between two grayish blots.

So, for the first five nights, looking up at the colored light show seemed a perfect distraction. But then came the moment when a black woman in a blue uniform appeared on all our screens and we learned we weren't alone in the universe. This small woman with her medals and shining braid, her jaw quivering oh so slightly, told us that the lights in the sky were visitors from no one knew where. I was on a city street when she came on and not a soul moved away from a screen anywhere along the blocks of sidewalk that I could see. She seemed to be trying to make her explanation as technical as possible, perhaps thinking we would becomes lost in her words and so not immediately feel the fear she knew she was piling on top of that we all were already feeling. Translated into the vernacular, it came down to this: the streaks we were seeing had been scanned and scanned again, measured and analyzed along every bit of spectrum we could tap into. They were not only coming down at night, but just as many were falling during the day when we couldn't see them for the sunlight. We weren't sure if these spheres were spacecraft, or machines of some order, with their sizes ranging from compact car to tugboat scale, but we knew now that they were appearing just beyond the furthest limits of our atmosphere—literally "appearing," in that they suddenly just popped into existence—and then free-falling toward us until the friction of their entry burned them to dust that then floated down toward the earth.

"So," I thought, "I have aliens in my hair."

You didn't have to be a dissociate to jump to the conclusion, then, that the mystery disappearances were alien abductions, and for days this was the odds-on favorite. But there were problems with the alien theory: "If they're advanced enough to build something that can pop in and out of space, bring them across billions of miles to snatch people up into their ships, do you really think they would neglect to build in some way to *stop*?" Like so much of what has happened, many of our questions about the disintegrating aliens were both terrifying and ludicrously funny. This whirl, this twist of emotional wires, fear wrapped around laughable absurdity, has since become the human norm. And I, for one, find that I'm now pretty comfortable with it.

Mathematics, as I said, is a machine: once started it runs itself to a logical conclusion. No such machinery was able to lead us to the truth about the burning aliens; the steps were erratic, the clues like skipping stones. Science took on the task of driving fine-tuning straight through the middle of fine-tuning, like an arrow splitting an arrow already in a bulls eye. It was determined—in the few minutes between the time the objects popped so suddenly into existence and their disintegration, all traced by radio spectrometers and mobility particle sizers—that the objects were spinning when they popped in, and it appeared there was indeed life in them, of some kind—the same long-string polymers based on the same amino acid building blocks that, as we all knew from elementary school, made up our own bodies. But nothing identifiably human registered in the readings. Whether these things had an outside and an inside or appeared and disintegrated as shell-less wholes no one could say for certain. These strangers appeared at first only in a thin slice of the night sky, but gradually the time stretched out to almost nine hours, contracted again, and they were gone. Seven months later they came back, streaking into the atmosphere against every constellation, and they never left. And we shivered: if every sector of the sky was throwing something at us did that mean that every part of space was unified in some cosmic grudge, all mounting some interstellar effort against us? The idea would have made Ptolemy proud, but unnerved us world-wide. We didn't want to be that special.

In the end it wasn't science that finally supplied a possible answer to what was happening in the over-head half of this double mystery, a possibility we then clung to. It was psychology 101: simple projection. A chess-player out pacing a soccer field after losing a championship match crooked her neck at the sky over Reykkavik one white night and said, "Sjalfsvig."

And, while there was of course no real evidence to support the idea, it somehow felt right. Somehow, from the moment we first heard of her suggestion that these bright streaks might be suicides, that life forms we knew nothing about, likely shared nothing with, were coming here—dozens of them a day—to deliberately burn themselves up in our atmosphere, we all felt this was likely the truth. "Lemming Excursion Modules," one shaky AM radio voice quipped. This was quickly shortened to the handier "Lems" and entered our common Armageddon parlance.

The idea was so shocking, spoke of such a sad and desperate mindset, that we didn't for a time notice how much things were changing in our own collec-tive psychology, didn't see that the insight of that chess player alone in the dark was a sign that some particular psychological traits had been ratcheted up in a good number of people all over the world. Marcella, for one; as I watched her it seemed obvious to me that she had become something of a savant at reading the interior landscape of others' minds. It often seemed as if she were able to zero in on what we were thinking and feeling just by looking at us. I did my best to keep my distance. When we sat down after the bus rodeo to at the bonfire of pallet wood and stacked waxed cups—its whitish smoke mingling with the black smoke of the smoldering busses—I sat on the opposite side of the fire from her. We all shared a celebratory feast of Jiffy-Pop and Slim Jims, except Bo who preferred his usual fare, rye bread and spearmint gum.

Dully and Mean Jean taunted one another.

"Of course, I wasn't an armored vehicle driver, as you were," Dully said.

"Are all veterinarains gutless, or just you?"

"On the contrary, I couldn't have been a veterinarian if I wasn't a brave man."

"Oh, those fierce little kittens!"

"Not the animals; their owners. Once a woman brought in her overfed cat and wanted me to give it something to keep it from eating the fancy grass in her fancy terrarium. 'It won't listen to me when I tell it no,' she said. I told her, 'The cat eats grass because the cat knows its needs grass, the same way a cow knows it needs to lick salt. The cat knows what it needs. You're the one who is not listening!' I was more afraid for my life during that fifteen minutes than I was seeing you drive your bus straight at me. Never underestimate the courage of a veterinarian."

"Or of a dentist," Todd said.

I shrugged.

"I'm not brave," Bo said. "I'm not brave at all. I'm afraid of machines, like Alistair is."

"Who said I'm afraid of machines?"

"You carry that little one around with you, and I see you take it out and look at it almost every night after we all go to bed, but you never turn it on. So you're afraid of it."

I hadn't told anyone about the cook-offs I'd seen, and I certainly hadn't told them about the inspector's palm deputy. "I found it, Bo. I don't turn it on because it's personal code protected. If I can ever figure out the code to unlock it, I promise you I won't be afriad to turn it on." I felt this was a fairly smooth transition from lying to telling the truth.

"Everything is a machine, Bo," Dully said. "Take this tea cup, for instance." He held up a graceful china cup he'd found at the prison and had been carrying with him ever since. "Near the brim it is very wide, so there is a lot of surface area for the tea to cool, so you can drink some tea right away. But as the cup goes down it narrows, so there is less surface area, and the tea cools slower. This tea cup is a machine for keeping tea at a constant temperature."

"No, I mean the other kind of machines: computers, electric motors, the kinds that suck us in and kill us."

"Kill us," Syd said.

Marcella, without lifting her head, said, "Shut the hell up Bo, or I'll switch your nuts for your tonsils." Her voice was calm, even musical, as she said it.

"Nuts for tonsils," Syd said.

"'Atta girl," Marcella said. "It's never too early to lay down a few ground rules."

"Alright, I won't say that. But can I say that I'm a little

disappointed in us? We've all been telling ourselves for years now, 'The machines will revolt! The machines are evil, they'll take over the world,' making bad movies about it ever since the day the first machine was invented." He laughed amiably. "And we still let it happen just like we all said it would. I'd had always hoped for some more original..."—he hesitated—"... demise, I guess...."

"Like filling up on root beer barrels and toppling over the falls," Marcella said.

"Seemed original."

"But you bungled the demise part."

"Why should I bother when I can get a machine to do it for me?"

Marcella buttoned Syd's pajamas and sat her down on a blanket where she immediately began stacking her shoes on top of Marcella's. Marcella began to serenade her:

> Tell my lovely little playmates
> That I never more will play.
> Give them all my toys, but mother,
> Put my little shoes away.

Dully leaned toward me and in a low voice said, "When a songbird learns a new song it is to attract a new mate. It grows new brain cells—notice," he said, holding up an index finger, "not an aesthetic instinct but one of long-term survival is behind song."

"I'll miss this place," Todd was saying. He had been living at the track before our group happened upon it.

He had said that he had been there since the cook-offs began, since he could no longer be a dentist, but—and I suspected he meant this to help defuse the tension between Bo and Marcella—he began to fill us in on some parts of his history that he had skipped over before.

"My practice was in Bad Axe, up in the thumb," Todd began, "and one day I had a patient cook-off right under me. He and I were talking about how different people have different thresholds of pain. He sat quietly for half a minute and then my burr was grinding air over a damp spot in the chair. I made myself go to work the next day, but not a single appointment showed up. The power went off mid-morning, so I drove back home. My wife was gone, but she'd been thoughtful enough to leave a note: 'I'd rather disappear in the rapture with Matt than sit in the dark with you.'"

"'The rapture?' Wow. So, who's Matt?" Marcella asked. She was settling Syd for sleep and she spoke softly.

"He worked for the Salvation Army. I used to make a big donation every year."

Mean Jean started to laugh, almost choking on her beer, and Dully laughed, too; Marcella grinned a crooked grin and shook her head. The rest of us kept straight faces.

"What did you do next?" Bo said, his eyes wide.

"I had a '39 Willys coupe, chopped four inches, frenched headlights, that I used to race at Milan Dragway; a beautiful *machine*, Indigo with a cat-shit-slick clear coat. It was the only beautiful thing left at the house. So I got in her and drove to Milan. Lived on peanuts and warm soda for a few weeks; slept in the manager's office. There was a divan, but it was loaded with fake I.D.s from underage girls and torn condom wrappers—"

"Been there," Mean Jean said.

"—so I slept on the floor on some loose seat cushions," Todd continued.

"Been there," Marcella said.

"I used to go down in the stands each day and try to reenact in my memory the best races I'd seen. Speeding cars always cheered me up."

"Been there," Bo said.

"But this time what had always made me happy just made me sad."

"Still there," I thought.

"Why are men always such more morose drunks?" Marcella said. Dully stood up and went off to find his prayer mat. "They can learn to hold their liquor, but not to hold their self-pity, have you noticed?" she asked Mean Jean. Mean Jean just grinned and opened another E&B.

"Drag strips are one-way and they lead to dead ends," Todd went on. "How's that for morose?" He was smiling. "Anyway, when I finally got into my car to leave, it was just too lonely to be in there all by myself; I had to get back out. That was when I found out it was impossible to be alone in a car anymore. So I started walking. East seemed as good a direction as any." He took off his glasses, rubbed his eyes. "A couple of days later I found this place. Spying the sign I told myself that an oval track wouldn't be such a parable, you know? I told myself it wouldn't be depressing, that an oval says something completely different from a straightaway to a dead end. And then, when I came in and saw that it was a figure—"

There was a sudden, sharp sizzling as one side of the fire was splashed with a thin wash of glycerin.

* * * * * * *

When we packed up the next morning, Marcella loaded Syd into the silver box of an old walk-behind lawn spreader that had been outfitted with pillows and a pink robe tie for a safety belt. The rest of us packed our things into a motley set of wheeled farm and garden implements and we set off between the still-smoking busses. Mean Jean was acting even cockier than usual, bragging about the way she'd treated us all as crash dummies the night before; Todd's disappearance had been the first time that she and the others in the group had witnessed a cook-off first hand. Dully had an expression on his face that I can only call "hunter's-eye;" he was as sharp as a hawk in the morning air. Marcella rarely feels dubious enough about herself that she has to lead, and despite the shock she'd surely felt the night before, that morning was no exception. And Bo? Well, Bo was a special case; we'd unanimously agreed to place him far, far down the duty roster of possible leaders, right below Syd. In the end, the turning of the wheels fell that morning to me.

When I first thought to take up with the Llull machine I was still bedding down with the slave servers in the industrial park behind my think tank. The way they tirelessly twittered away in the name of layered repetition was somehow comforting; Mama's heartbeat in a digital key, the heat sinks silver fingers of reliable warmth. So much of the net was drowning in panic that this, the taproot of the information tree, was the only place I felt able to tap unpolluted information. I spent the night hours there, reading mathematics texts to keep my mind off the colorful deaths high above me. But this had its hazards, as well. One evening I was sipping a *Guinness* (most tech people worked in a drunken state in those in-between days; something below the level of decision, some instinct told us this was the path to follow) and as I read "in these experiments the sign '=' may stand for the words 'is confused with,'" I felt a flush begin spreading across my throat. It may well have been the *Guinness*, but I was sure it was the onset of a cook-out. I threw the book across the room and shouted as loudly as I could: "Mathematics is a perfectly logical system without flaw!" I immediately felt cooler. Thanks be to Gödel.

Panicky, drunken researchers had been diligently rooting through bios and digital tracers around the world and, as the last of the coherent broadcasts led me to understand, the signs indicated that intense, clear thinking may—they repeated the *may*—have some correlation to the cook-offs. The arbitrary, the confused, the blindly zealous were all still very much among us. Sitting there, the beads of cold sweat on my forehead bigger than the beads of damp on the bottle, I first felt the loop: I decided I had to find a way to act arbitrarily—but could I deliberately determine how to act arbitrarily? I was bound to slip up; I could never be certain that I wouldn't accidentally fall into logic. Like every man in every dark space at least since Neanderthal Man had crouched in the Black Forest, I saw that I would need a tool if I were to survive.

I downed three more *Guinness* as fast as I could, and was transported back to my university days: I remembered the chipped seminar tables, and then I remembered Ramón Llull. Llull was a thirteenth-century genius who thought that religious and philosophical ideas should be combined, but that simple rationality was too limited to accomplish it. He invented a machine with concentric wheels, each with a series of symbols drawn on it. When the wheels were wound around, different ideas lined up with one another and the operator then set about trying to understand how they went together—as a religious man, Llull was sure that everything indeed went with everything else, that we just had to keep trying, keep turning and divining until we understood. And Llull, in his tight focus on the directives of the Divine had, just outside his peripheral vision, as it were, produced a wonderfully human instrument—that is, an instrument to keep us human. It was the perfect idea for the new reality: technologically primitive, aleatorically advanced.

Llull's machine was made of pasteboard, and I built my first one from printer paper box-lids using a pair of pinking sheers that mysteriously dangled on a string from above the console. It had two sets of two wheels, and all the edges having been cut with pinking sheers gave the device a cheery air—a combination of sampler and shiny little gears. Llull's original thinking machine was a complete diagram, or so Llull intended, of the attributes of his God. Llull put the letter A at the center, and the letters B through K in nine sections (Llull's original language had no use for "J") out near the edge of the circle. Each letter had its own attribute from B for goodness, to K for glory, and all the letters were connected to one another by spidery lines—a taut, symmetrical needlepoint making up a star and some polygons that connected all the points of the King of Eternity. This was the ancestor of the Magic 8-Ball, of the young girl's "Cootie-Catcher" that sucks in questions like a dry anemone, a relic from the times before our childhoods' faith in chance and fate stumbled and the devolution to logic began to set in.

I kept Llull's number of pie slices—nine has always seemed a serious number to me—but cut the number of wheels to four, giving me thirty-six slots for words or phrases and two centers to fill. I replaced Llull's transcendent guiding ideas with safer, less inspiring ones, the first set too accurately reflecting my state of mind:

Hesitate
Sou-westerly
Eat

Sleep
Left-ish
Cellar Door
Walls
Don't Complain
Shoot

(I didn't have a weapon, but like everyone else I had absorbed dozens of gleeful 3-D post-apocalyptic sagas, and such preconceptions were hard to shake),

Don't Look Up
Move

I grimaced at the indecisive, sloppy vocabulary I'd chosen in that first round, and tried to tight things up with a list from my profession. It was surprisingly difficult to find terms with any practical application. I wrote in,

Invert
Multiply
Sine
Cosine

(these last two I figured could be read phonetically),

Divide
Mean

This last I knew could be read in at least two ways. I wistfully erased some of the truest poetry of topology, "monotone decreasing path," "orbifold," "Lie group" (named for S. Lie), and "local extrema," although their utility in planning routes through physical space were so obvious. I knew they wanted to be on the list, but I erased them because I didn't plan on telling anyone what I had been, or what I had been doing. This didn't seem the best time to be a guru of abstract mathematics, nor to have had my degree of intimacy with two cook-offs.

I next put down a string of the kinds of small words that have Velcro at each end, the ones that do all the work of making sense, small words like "and," "across," and the others. The rest I filled in with words chosen at random—or at least as random as I could make them, choosing "Wichita" and "wire," "rerouting" and "heat sink," and a few more from the index of a tech manual by the servers, and—the last thing I entered in the slots—"tighten your nuts," from a pinup calendar I'd found hanging on the back wall.

In the center of both pairs of wheels I lettered the same thing in a circle, "Reverse Yourself." I wanted to always have that option dead center.

Countering insane times with randomness and absurdity isn't a new idea; philosophers and drug addicts have always had them in their toolboxes. Just over a century ago, for one, the terrible insanities of the First World War were met by the deliberate insanities of artists; other wars have inspired other groups.

But the Dadaists and the Yippies were as powerless as goldfish at the top of a spoiled tank, gasping for life, trying to break down their surroundings and infuse a little oxygen by having their surreal tales pass over their civilization's gills. Funny hats, howling poems of animal noises, an agenda of insulting the audience, fast dancing with architecture. Too little, too stagey. I had no ambitions about saving civilization; I only wanted to be able to cross the city without being reduced to a shallow glycerin sheen. I would turn the wheels and make my own connections, cobble together my own explanations—and whatever else they might be they certainly wouldn't be a mathematician's logic.

But my first outing, in search of food (and of companions, which I inexplicably also found I wanted, a desire dizzying in its novelty), letting myself be guided by the slight papery hiss of the spinning wheels led to a bad end. *Sine / Wire / Left-ish / Don't Complain* were the words the wheels offered me. I stepped out of the door of the slave room and there, directly across the parkway, was a sign on a wire fence, slightly to my left. I took a startled step back—I felt as if something had been eavesdropping on me. But it was simply a reminder of how difficult it is to make our minds do something truly random; we would always revert to what we knew, always try to make sense of the random, and as my office window looked out over this parkway, I certainly knew this sign. But as—less surprisingly—I saw nothing that might match the last phrase, I felt encouraged. The sign read *Traffic Circle*

Ahead. I walked in that direction. The last building I had to pass before the traffic circle was a theatre. The marquee read *Isadora Duncan: Selections.*

As I passed under the marquee, the theatre doors crashed open and four large men stepped out; they blocked my path, surrounded me. The four wore matching work clothes; a union patch was sewn on over the pocket of each of their shirts. They must have been stagehands, the crew who pulled the ropes and wired the lights and dragged the castles back and forth, but they were all wearing pink caps. A patch on the front of the caps bore silhouettes of dancers and the name of the theatre—but they were pink. They moved closer and I struggled, but I couldn't help myself: a short bark of laughter escaped me—pink! When I awoke, I found they had torn the Llull Machine into small pieces and possibly broken the little finger of my left hand but that was all. Still, I sat in the doorway of the dark slave room all evening staring up at the Lems, trying not to complain, but still feeling sorry for myself. I imagined it was a big club.

The next day I walked in the opposite direction from the slave room and found a wide-open flea market. On a dusty back table I found antiques: jackets and sleeves for vinyl LPs and 45s, insert booklets for lost CDs. With the help of some white paint and some black nail polish I found there, I started making another Llull Machine (the little finger the rabble the day before had broken only slowed me a little). There was a record player at the table, but no power in the building. I hunted around and found a pencil with a good stiff eraser and a pack of sewing needles. I pushed the thickest of the needles through the eraser at an angle, clamped the wooden part of the pencil between my teeth, set the needle in the grooves of one of the 45s and spun the turntable by hand—I could hear the music through my teeth. I sampled maybe a dozen then built my new Llull machine on one slow song and one fast, both 45s from the *Fortune* label: "Bacon Fat" by Andre Williams, and "Industrial Breakdown," by "Dr. Isaiah Ross, the Harmonica Boss." I used most of the same words over again, but tried to rectify a few oversights—"run," and "hide" being prominent among these—and kept the reversal option phrase in the center of each pair.

All this time, my brethren had been grinding on, in that slow but exceedingly fine way we all cultivated, and while nothing more was learned about the Lems, another correlation became visible, if only dimly. Because the amounts were so small, so the disclaimers ran, nothing was certain, but it appeared that when someone near a self-repairing machine of any kind was cooked-off, trace amounts of some minerals were mysteriously added to the feeders in the machine's self-repair cartridge kits. The amounts discovered were never the same from machine to machine, nor were the materials found.

So emerged the rather old-fashioned theory that the machines were taking us apart, efficiently sorting our elements by atomic weight, and adding us to their stores: we were the grasshoppers, they were the ants.

But because the main source for all refill units were the pollution skimmers clustered on the roofs, ten-foot high loops of filaments that, glowing like lantern mantels inside a lantern glass, scrubbed carbon and any other particles out of the city air and channeled it into the cartridges, no one could be certain.

Despite that uncertainty, power stations all over the world immediately browned down to an intermittent flicker of a few dirty volts. The utility crews worried they were aiding in their own eventual destruction. The generators and transformers and all the rest were left intact, as huge and still as the heads on Easter Island, but no one dared to awaken them. With that, I decided to leave the silent slaves behind and move...? East, I decided, for no reason other than that was where the sun came up. My face would dry faster.

CHAPTER THREE

WE MEMBERS OF OUR off-to-see-the-Wizard-style group, drastically different personalities linked together by confusion, moving along the now-empty roads, had seemed to gather one another like burrs, just by passing through fields—fields of fellow wanderers, that is.

Only a few days after leaving the city I was sitting on a hill overlooking a church on a two-lane road. I was eating chow mein noodles out of a can, and I heard a loud metallic whirring sound. It was someone riding a Taylor One-Wheel, coming down slope. The rider pulled up at the planter in front of the church and turned off the One-Wheel's engine. He took off his goggles and sat on the edge of the planter, eating his lunch, and looking up at the signboard in the center of the planter. The sign read

YES!
WE'RE HANGING ON
TO A SOLID ROCK!

When he was finished eating, the rider stepped into the planter and pulled all the letters off the sign. He began rearranging them—*WE CHAOS DARE,* he put up, then took back down; *SHREWED YANKEE* didn't last, either. In the end he settled for:

K O ANY NOIR LEADER
GOING WEST!!

He still had letters left in his hand, and he stuck them down in the bottom right corner: *COSH*. That's when I walked down and introduced myself to Kyle.

He and I found Whiteman trying to spear pigeons with a ski pole, and Mean Jean (I didn't learn her real name, Genevieve de la Vega, until she and Kyle became a sometimes couple, and he began calling her "Genevieve Day"), just drove up to us one afternoon, on an Amigo as draped with chains as Marley's Ghost. Todd and Dully were already at the abandoned prison when we found it. It was one of the few places big enough for such a small handful of people to be able to move into. This was another of the odd global twists in human psychology: no one wanted to be alone, but the smaller the group, the larger any enclosed gathering place had to be. There was a kind of remedy, though, man's oldest—any number, large or small, could sit comfortably around an open fire. But to move in out of the rain a band as small as ours needed a barn-sized— or prison cafeteria-sized—space.

One afternoon, when we were all gathered in the prison workshop, making hawk-sized paper airplanes from the loose pages of the Braille books the prisoners had been contracted to make, we saw approaching two shimmering, contorted dust devils that appeared to be made entirely of light. Marcella and Syd had found us, having walked away from a deserted kids' summer camp on the hottest day of the year, their forms shimmering on the hot cement as they came through the open gates.

We were all more or less happy in the prison all that winter and into spring, and then one morning, against all laws of probability that I knew, all the Llull cues insisted as one that we should move along. It made no sense to leave our comfortable prison, but none of us were willing to risk doing the sensible thing. (Only Marcella didn't vote; she shook her head and went to bathe Syd in the pot from one of the giant pressure cookers in the kitchen. She had her own purposes in life, and it didn't matter to her where she dropped her pack.) We moved out that afternoon, set off east, along the musically named Oakville Waltz Road, and three dawns later we found Flat Rock, and with it Todd.

Now, with Flat Rock behind us, we were headed northeast in a long parabolic curve, avoiding the heart of Sink DT. It had been the biggest Load Center in the Great Lakes District before it morphed into the epicenter of the Ruin Porn movement; a city ahead of its time. By all accounts (the power grid might go down; the rumor grid abides; we weren't the only wandering band, and we had hosted several as they passed through, some heading due east, some northeast, some southeast), the deranged and violent flourished there, happily, thrashing against one another like fish in too narrow a channel. Our faith in the protective power of the arbitrary meant we would keep wandering until we found the answers to "wire" with "three," "listen" with "right hand," and "don't" with "climb." If we ever found them, perhaps we would flourish, too. When these word pairs spun up as we paused with our packs beneath the jet-black ocarina, I had to shake my head: where again had I gotten the idea to use the Llull Machine, why had I, out of nowhere, remembered this flimsy device from a long-ago class on the History of Combinatronics. It's in the character of an oracle to speak in riddles; of a prophet to speak in tongues. And the cardboard and vinyl's chatter was no more upfront. Why couldn't the idea of using the I Ching have come to me instead? That comes with a tried and true guide book. Numbers on dice would have been more amenable to nudges in interpretation, and might have made all our uncertainties seem part of one big Vegas Night. It seems that, addicted to passive processes as I have always been, I've never developed much in the way of foresight—and foresight was the one thing that could have actually helped us. I laughed, again: it was all so hilarious and terrifying, again.

As we usually did when we were traveling, we built a fire on the rumble strips near the edge of the expressway. About an hour before we stopped, Pauli had suddenly gone running down the embankment of the freeway, and when he returned he had had two chickens whose necks he had snapped. This prompted Bo to chime in with, "A chicken is only an egg's way of making another egg. You'll notice the eggs have escaped. The ringleaders always do." I appreciated Bo's circular nonsense; he reminded me of a biologist I'd worked with named Sol. Sol insisted that "Nucelic acids invented human beings in order to be able to reproduce themselves even on the moon."

Chickens were at the top of the food chain; coincident with the cook-offs and the arrival of the Lems something had happened to water—even that from the deepest of wells or gathered from the rain somehow no longer matched the water in our cells, something in its nature had changed such that "water" wasn't "water" anymore. It looked and tasted fine, there were no parasites or bacteria in it, but fresh water would now tear a person's insides into shreds, double him or her over for days. Instead of seeping into the cells and keeping us healthy—the millennia-long human/water contract—the new water tore things out of the cells.

The process of osmosis, despite being as passive as they come, is a double-edged sword. It can be both vital and destructive. Plants can't live without its commerce through their cells walls, and we can't live without its wicking of fluids through membranes, but it's also why we can't drink salt water if we're shipwrecked: the cells draw in the salt and push out the water, dehydrating themselves. You would think this would prove once and for all that the confederationists have it all wrong, that individual cells clearly have no consciousness of their own, no intelligence. But then, the bobbing jelly-bodied siphonophore of cells we call the brain knows no better, either—it continually draws in any foreign operations it encounters, aspires to the wicking up of the detached chemistry of caesium and cybernetics like a worshipful younger brother imitating a brilliant sister, hoping to push out the unpredictable sums of the human algorithms in the process. In the end, a single cell in one of our kidneys is no dumber than the brain itself.

So, we drank only harvested bottled drinks now, and squeezed cider in the fall, tapped maple trees in the spring. As the cook-offs and the animal entrapments of the sinks had severely thinned the suburban population we had no trouble finding enough to drink. But the mysteriously denatured water had killed off all the freshwater fish (though we heard that saltwater life survived), it killed off all the cats and dogs and horses, even the pigs. Drinking more than a few drops of fresh water doomed anything with a brain larger than a marble, but the chickens and rabbits and squirrels drank it with no side effects, and when we hunted and ate them the meat didn't make us sick; it was as if their bodies, like the apples and cherries and grapes that grew across the state, transformed the water back into a safe form. Just one more mystery among many.

We were eating late because of the time it took for Pauli to ready the chickens for cooking. Marcella and Syd were playing, Mean Jean was polishing her boots, and I was fooling with the palm deputy again, still with no luck. We still had Todd on our minds, so no one in our group wanted to talk much that night. So, in one of those balancing coincidences that our new reality made seem so normal and yet so ominous, the night produced someone who did.

"Hello, the camp!"

Mean Jean looked off to the north. "Incoming," she said.

The man who approached us displayed a big smile through an even bigger beard. It billowed a foot below his collar line. He walked with a wooden cane in his right hand and he carried an orange string bag in his left. His beard and his very short hair were white, his skin a light coffee color.

"Good evening," he said, with a brief, gasping laugh. "I'm Rich. As in, uh uh, short for Richard, that is. I wonder, might I, uh uh, *share* your fine fire for a time?" His voice was somewhat high-pitched, his manner a campfire version of courtly. The gasp in his laugh was not because he was out of breath.

He didn't sit, but leaned against the guardrail a few yards down from Mean Jean.

Dully had been down the embankment, praying his *witr* in a grove of staghorn sumac. Carrying his prayer rug he came up almost directly behind Rich, who looked back over his shoulder. "Good evening," he said. "I imagine you don't, uh uh, drink alcohol, but would you care for some cheese?" Rich reached into his string bag and brought out a smaller string bag, this one with small circles of cheese in wax. "Perhaps you would like one for tomorrow?"

"If this means there is to be a tomorrow, then yes, thank you," Dully said, and he took one.

From out of the bag Rich next drew a bottle of wine. "I find that if I, uh uh, carry wine instead of perishables—so it's not just that I walk very slowly, as you see," (I was the only one who recognized this as a very dry joke)—"I can usually find someone willing to share a meal and a drink with me."

"You've come on a good night, Santa," said Bo. As usual, he wasn't so much simple as tangent-minded.

"It is a good night, yes," said Rich, laughing again, and running his hands through his beard. He looked into the shallow pan we had resting over the fire. "This fare is perfect, because...I also have here a small box of, uh uh, corn starch. Do you have another pan? Also, as my legs unfortunately don't scissor down and up very well any more, I will need a volunteer to tend the wine sauce for me."

I set another pan on the coals. While I was pouring the wine into it, Rich and the others continued talking. I missed the first part of the conversation, so I didn't know how they had travelled from wine sauce to the question of the cook-offs.

"And, while it is certainly true that those poor devils' minerals *appear* to have been absorbed into those nearby machines', uh uh, negentropy injectors in *some cases,* hardly proves that the machines *took* them. I spent more than thirty years as a maker of sand molds for custom casting. The hot metal indeed poured into the molds, but I never once, in that time, thought that the molds, the molds *themselves,* caused the metal to be poured, uh uh, into them." In the firelight we could see that his smile was different now; the center of his top lip was pulled down over the lower one. He looked from one of us to the others. "Correlation isn't causation, as I feel sure, quite sure, you all remember. And your unfortunate friend wasn't, uh uh, in a computer room, or near any machinery was he?"

"Dully says everything is a machine," Bo said, "even cups, even people and animals."

"That's certainly true enough. And, given *that* fact, we've all been disappearing and being absorbed by machines for the entire history of the world, haven't we? It's, uh uh, our biological fate, isn't it."

The sizzle of the chicken was the only sound for a long moment. I sat the wine bottle down on the pavement and Mean Jean snatched it up.

"So," said Rich, breaking the silence, "where are you all going?"

"Northeast," Marcella said. She was bouncing Syd on her lap. When we would encounter others, it was most often she who would take the part of the sour and suspicious one, but whatever she was feeling about Rich's sudden appearance at our fire it had erased her habitual scowl.

"Northeast; I see. No more precise destination?" He held the box of corn starch out to me. "Two table spoons and a sprinkle more should, uh uh, do it."

"Precision is overrated," Bo said. And even though I knew he was parroting back something he had heard me say, it made me like Bo even more.

"Wherever we are led," Dully said, and he looked at

me. I didn't think that any of our party would mention the Llull Machine, and Dully knew his words would most likely be taken as being religious, or fatalistic. Dully had been with our party since the prison, but he still had not completely reconciled himself to the use of the wheels. He worried that its use was somehow blasphemous, a blemish on his faith in Allah. I told him it had been based on an earlier device invented by the Arabs, but this didn't mollify him.

"Well," said Rich, crossing his arms over his chest, "That's fine. But as for *me,* I find I always need a destination or, uh uh, at least a goal. I'm not good with aimless wandering."

Marcella began to sing Syd a slow Cajun waltz:

I went coasting down the country
Let my mustang just run free
With the top down I smelled the Georgia pines
At Fat Tuesday I turned right
Stopped where oil fires light the night
And now as you can see I'm doing fine....
But I hear you say, "Oh, no, that ain't no real life!"
Moving with no reason's not your style
But I say it's quite all right,
To dance with Sister Chance once in a while

I'd noticed early on that Marcella seemed to know only songs that no one else had ever heard, and when she sang one, despite it almost always being as a song for Syd, who loved to hear her sing—the only thing, in fact, that made Syd smile—it seemed always to mirror the conversational point.

"I've heard good things about north, south and east," Rich said. "But I've heard nothing about the north-east. Do you suppose that that's a, uh uh, good sign? The silence of wide open spaces, maybe?" This time everyone recognized that Rich was at least half joking. The aromas of the warming wine and the simmering chicken were rising and filling the air and everyone seemed to relax a few degrees more than usual. I saw another Lem just above the horizon.

"You've heard good things about the east?" said Mean Jean. "That's where Sink DT is. There's nothing good over that way."

"Oh, on the contrary, on the contrary. And in fact that's, uh uh, my destination."

"Are you from there?"

"No; from Novi, just north of here."

Mean Jean took another drink from the wine bottle and passed it up to Pauli, who was standing behind her, only half-watching his chickens fry.

"Then why are you going there? It's a sink," Pauli said.

"Yes, indeed it is. And in fact, that's exactly the reason I'm going."

"And what do you think you will find in such a place?" asked Dully, who was still at the railing only a few feet away from him.

"Well," Rich shrugged. "Anything and everything that's there."

"That's crazy," said Bo, smiling.

"Have any of you here ever actually *been* to a sink?" Rich asked.

No one had. "We've heard the stories," Marcella said, in a tone that suggested there was nothing more to be said on the subject.

"Ah, stories!" said Rich and he laughed his gasping laugh again. "I love stories. Books, movies, people sitting around a fire—all kinds of stories."

"I like comics," Pauli said.

"As do I," answered Rich, his voice swooping from low to high. "I can still tell you the plots of some of the Superman comics I read when I was a boy. And I particularly loved Bizarro comics: 'Do nothing perfect,' was their world's motto."

"Looks like they shared that with us," Dully said.

"Yes. I never thought I would grow *out* of Superman and *into* Bizarro's world!" He laughed at his own joke, but Pauli laughed harder. "Another favorite of mine," Rich said, "was the issue where Superman, uh uh, more or less spin-balances the earth by flying tons and tons of junk cars down to Antarctica and burying them in a pit? Because the northern and southern hemispheres are not equal in mass, you see, and the world was about to rip itself apart at the equator, or perhaps it was that it collapse on itself from the north down—as if the, uh uh, southern hemisphere were a skinny woman balancing a fat man on her shoulders and her knees were about to give out. I do certainly remember that Superman had to make all corners of the earth weigh the same so the world wouldn't explode. I remember wondering if there was an, uh uh, underlying Cold War message there. What do you think?"

I thought it was perfectly possible that as a young boy this cheerful, talkative old man had been capable of wondering about hidden Cold War messages in comic books. Clues can be found anywhere, if you're looking hard enough.

"I meant stories about Sink DT," Marcella said.

"Ah, yes. Well, I knew that. Excuse my, uh uh, digression. Well now, you've heard the stories, I've heard the stories, everybody has heard the stories." Rich leaned toward the fire. "I believe the sauce has thickened enough now, shall we pour out a little for everyone?"

Pauli passed pieces of chicken. Every one of us except Dully poured a little of the thick, cloudy sauce onto our plates to dip the chicken into.

"The heat makes all the alcohol evaporate, so you could have some if you'd like," Rich said to Dully, who only smiled and shook his head, then leaned forward to stoke up the fire as all the pans were off it now. "So, speaking of stories, what's the dinner time custom here?" Rich asked. "Does anyone want to tell us stories while we eat or do you prefer a, uh uh, *companionable* silence?" He ran his fingers through his beard again.

"You were going to tell us a story about the sinks," Pauli said.

"Was I? We'd decided? Maybe someone else should...?"

"That's what a sandman is supposed to do: tell stories," Marcella put in.

"Or do you think your wine and cheese is enough to trade for our company?" said Mean Jean, pointing a chicken leg at him. "And corn starch? We destroy school busses for fun."

"Oh, then of course the price of admission would indeed be higher here. Well, a story about sink DT, then. As we all now have remembered being preached into us in school, cities are about gathering resources together. And the, uh uh, people in cities share these resources, always in a kind of uneven balance, because there are always some who get more than others"

"And we were always 'the others,'" said Bo

Rich laughed his gasping laugh. "Yes, it may be that all of us here have always have been 'the others.' Be that as it may, when a city's resources are stretched too thin or population expands too much or, as is now the case, and for reasons unknown, too large a crowd gathers at one site, they pass a critical size and instead of spreading out, people from all over the area continue to gather in that one space and overwhelm the limits of the reward, whatever the reward may be there. It can be anything. And they ignore other less crowded areas that also have what they want or need. The population becomes obsessed with this one site, or a very few sites in the entirety of the city." He paused to take a few bites of his dinner.

"Were you a mold-maker-slash-teacher?" Marcella asked. From my angle, her eyes glowed like a cat's in the light from the fire.

"No. Slash talker and listener is all," Rich said. "And, more recently, slash, uh uh, *rememberer*. I first heard about these sinks in a high school psychology class." He laughed. "They had just been named at the time, so you know that was indeed a very, very long time ago. But since the cook-offs, since the Lems, it seems that my mind has brought everything it had ever absorbed up to the surface to see what might be of, uh uh, use. Huge amounts of memories have come back, all together, all at once." He shrugged.

"I know what you mean," Mean Jean said. "It happened to me, too. I remember everything I learned in basic, everything from every patrol." She smiled. "My best sex."

"Then you are so much luckier than I," Rich said with a laugh."My recall didn't bring back physical memories." He frowned. "I wonder why that should be. At any rate, back to the sinks. I remember that there is some, uh uh, change in the psychology of the people who enter such an area. It isn't the lack of space and resources elsewhere that keeps people together once this happens. Some overriding social need for the community members to interact with one another takes over past that, uh uh, tipping point, past some mysterious limit, and the old society breaks down, turns itself inside out—but still no one moves away; because that need to have *so much* interaction with others is a stronger need even than the, uh uh, need to survive. And that's what has happened in Sink DT and, I hear, in all big cities. Neighborhoods emptied as hundreds of people for no reason they could understand pushed their way into already crowded urban crannies, leaving miles of abandoned homes in perfectly livable areas, in a mad rush that overwhelmed the skimpy resources at the centers, because they felt the need to be packed in tight. It's both comforting and self-destructive—as, uh uh, is the way with so many social instincts, isn't it?"

I could see that Rich was having a fine time singing for his supper. A Lem flared up bright white and died in the sky over his and Dully's heads. Rich looked up and said, "Anyone else ever wonder if we now have aliens in our hair?" Pauli laughed.

"In a behavioral sink," Rich went on, "there are shortcomings, yes. People are more aggressive, they forget how to raise their children in their traditional way—there can even be infant cannibalism." He raised his eyebrows, then finished his dinner. "Many people die, of course, even as more rush to pile onto the heap; there is more mental illness, more disease of all sorts, more drug and alcohol abuse. Balancing this, at least for some, there is a lot of, uh uh, *creativity* in sexual practice."

"So a sink is just one group of pervs' way of making more pervs?" said Bo. He looked honestly curious.

"And what a wonderful world this *is*," said Rich. "The antidote to a sink is very simple: people could just spread out and interact less. And a healthy society, or at least a healthier one, would reemerge."

"So the best way to survive as a group," Marcella

said, "is to avoid contact with one another."

Rich was delighted by her. "Yes, exactly, exactly. But then, we all sort of knew that all along, didn't we?" He laughed again. "So it's hard to understand why a sink could ever form, isn't it? My teacher certainly didn't know!"

"People on their own tend to think more rationally," Dully said. He had been sitting silently for most of Rich's recital, impatience showing on his face.

"Which, these days, can be a bad thing," I said, looking straight at Dully.

Rich wasn't so delighted by me. But he nodded his head. "There certainly seem to be fewer and fewer places where it comes in handy."

"A sink isn't one of them," Dully said.

"No, it seems not. But at least I know where I'm going and what I'm looking for." He didn't add that this was more than we were doing, but we all heard it.

The fire had died down to a web of embers and Mean Jean rolled out her salvaged rubber raft. Flipped upside down it made an oval hammock on the ground. She pushed it a few yards down the shoulder, stretched out on it and pulled a blanket over her legs.

"You're free to stay by our fire," Pauli said. We had all noticed that other than his string bag and his cane, Rich carried only what looked like a rolled up beach towel tied with old clothes line rope gone gray, strung over his shoulder.

"Well, thank you, but I need to, uh uh, be on my way." He lifted his string bag and shouldered his slim bedroll.

"You have someplace special to be, do you?" Mean Jean asked.

Rich laughed his gasping laugh as he used his cane to lever himself onto his feet. "I hope so. I just don't know where yet."

"What are you looking for?"

Rich smiled shyly. "Some not overly nice young man who will offer to share his blankets with me. Just as a bottle of, uh uh, salvaged wine is usually enough to get me invited to dinner, a thin bedroll and an honest show of interest are usually enough to get me sex." He lifted his cane in a farewell wave. "I enjoyed our talk." None of us said a word as he walked past the end of the guardrail and started down the embankment. There was a rattle of sliding gravel. "That wasn't me," Rich called back, and he was gone.

"Well," Dully said.

Pauli stood looking into the dark for a long moment, then turned and asked us, "What's the answer? What *are* we trying to find?" But he wasn't really asking the questions. He picked up his pack and his blanket and sprinted off down the bank, calling out as he ran, "Rich! Wait."

"I cried because I had no direction, until I met a man who told me I had no sex," Bo said.

And then we were six.

CHAPTER FOUR

D<small>ULLY AND</small> B<small>O WANDERED</small> away to find places to bed down, but Marcella took my arm before I could do the same.

"Sit by the fire with me," she said, "while I sing to Syd. Syd likes this next song because we get to pound things, don't we, Syd? It's ...'Wonderful Widow.'" The little girl began to slap out a clumsy rhythm on the clutter of toys in front of her. Marcella grinned and began singing a slow, loose lyric: *"night by silent sailing night...."*

I had heard her sing this song before, but it seemed more haunting each time, and Marcella sang the beautiful but strange lyric—Edgar Allan Poe could have written many of the lines—with more assurance than she sang any of the other songs.

"That's beautiful," I said when she was done.

Syd was bored now, and went off to play with the laces in her spare pair of shoes.

"Do you...," Marcella began slowly. "Do you have memory problems?"

"Sometimes I forget where I put my keys—a year and a half ago."

She shook her head. "That's...I'm not talking about lost memories. I'm talking about memories that are *too* present; pushy memories. Memories like Rich was talking about." I noticed that when she began a sentence she would tilt her head slightly to the side, and straighten it again when she'd finished. Then I realized that she was expecting me to say something.

"All that about the Bizarro comics and about the sinks? It was odd that he would remember all that."

"I know maybe a hundred songs, like everybody does. But every night just after sundown 'The Wonderful Widow of Eighteen Springs' pushes itself on me. It's like the other ninety-nine are outside, and I can see them through a window, but 'The Wonderful Widow' is inside with me, demanding my attention."

"Everyone gets songs stuck in their heads; jingles."

"I understand that...." she said, each word evenly spaced, keeping her temper with me. I was irritating her by not understanding what she was trying to say. "Stop looking away and listen, Alastair. This is something else, and I'm talking to you about it because I think that you'd be likely to tell me the truth if you've felt something like it." She was right. "And I think this is something important, but I don't know what it is. Look up, look at me and listen, OK? I only heard that song once, Alastair, years ago at a concert I didn't want to go to, a concert I hated."

"It obviously made a big impression."

"Oh, it impressed me, alright. An Asian woman sitting at a closed piano, pounding on the wood of it with her hands, never once touching the keys; another woman standing there, singing the words like they were opera and the pounding woman was her orchestra. I was sure God was punishing me for going out with someone who wasn't a jock."

"God's on the side of the jocks?"

She stretched her arms out wide. "He loves us! We do the most for his image." Then her smile faded. "But now, just since everything started to fall apart, I want to sing that song every night. No, no...*it* wants me to sing it every night. Sometimes I sing other songs just to push it aside. Do you feel anything like that?"

I'd never before had this extended an exchange with Marcella. "I have," I said.

"Well?" She opened her eyes wide and stared at me.

"About the Llull Machine," I said. "I've wondered why, out of nowhere, I remembered it from a History of Combinatronics class I'd snored through."

"I don't know what combinatronics is. And I've never really been sure what an actuary is, for that matter."

"Combinatronics is just specialized mathematics. It's nothing. It's used in computer science, to create some formulas, to work with algorithms." I was trying not to sound like what I was.

"And you just remembered it out of nowhere, the way I remembered 'The Wonderful Widow,' and Rich remembered about the behavior sink." It wasn't a question. Marcella lowered her voice. "Sometimes I can tell what ideas are going through people's heads just by looking at them."

"I've noticed. You're a highly empathetic woman."

"Look at me, Alistair. No; into my eyes." She swore, exasperated. "Okay, let's get this out of the way so we can talk: I know I make you drool; I get that. But it's best that you put that aside, understand?" She began to sing:

> *What you've never had*
> *You can't miss*
> *You won't crave*
> *Or think about,*
> *It can't get you*
> *Sweating blood*
> *Or climbing*
> *Up the wall,*
> *But what you've once had*
> *You want again*
> *That*
> (she clapped her hands twice, softly)
> *Everyday*
> *It breaks your heart*
> *From the day it starts*
> *That sweet good thing....*

"But I need you to concentrate for me, Alistair, I need to see your face while I talk this through. Clear enough?"

My neck felt like as tight as a rusty hinge when I nodded. I tried to push away my embarrassment by doing some calculus—"Even when dy/dx = 0/0, dy/dx *doesn't* = 0 because the differential relation still exists *as a relation*"—but it was no help.

"Good. Because I think this is important. First, I don't have any special empathy for people, not in the way people you mean, for feelings. Anybody could guess yours, so that doesn't count. What I do have is empathy for their *ideas*. Do you understand what I'm trying to say?"

She leaned forward, her long curls brushed my hand and I said, "What?"

"Listen to me: I look at people and I don't see what they're feeling, but I do see what they're thinking, how they're ordering things in their head, see the ideas they're having, or *hosting*, maybe. Okay?"

"Hosting? You make it sound like ideas are parasites."

"Gold star. But listen. It's not a precise thing, but what I can see is clear enough that I know that none of us here think alike. It's not just that we don't have the same ideas, but that the *way* each of us think is completely different from everyone else. It's like we're a box of mixed chocolates, or a set of gears set up to mesh at just one point and drive something, or...." She shook her head in frustration. "This is hard for me to explain, and do you know why, Alistair? Because it's new. This isn't how I was before the cook-offs and the Lems and the rest, when my deepest thought was how to improve my swing for my next softball game. I had a touch of it—I've always been able to read pitchers really well, and I can tell a lot about a child just by the way she stands—had it the way you might have a touch of the flu. But now it's taken over; it's trying to become all that I am. So, ya, it's like a parasite. Do you understand what I'm trying to say?"

I did. "I do. As if all the cards in your personal deck have been shuffled into a new hand and you're being told how to play it."

Marcella grasped my knee. "Exactly! Alistair, thank you! But why do you think this is happening?"

"Stress; the collapse of our world as we knew it is bound to change us, disorient us."

"Maybe," she said, but she was shaking her head again. "But I don't think so. If that was it wouldn't we reshuffle things to help us survive all this with a little more security? Is wandering the roads, sitting around campfires in the open instead of staying in a place where we were comfortable really a smart reaction to that kind of stress? Why did we leave the track, Alistair?"

"Because we'd been there long enough, I suppose."

"You know that makes no sense."

"I still say that making sense is dangerous."

"I know. But there are millions of ways to not make sense. If that's what it was about, why would we all have the same idea—or the same idea have us—at the same time?" She was getting more and more upset as she tried to talk her way through her questions.

"I'm sorry, Marcella, but I just don't see what you're driving at. Maybe I'm too tired."

"Just give me a few more minutes, or—I'm giving you fair warning—I'll wake you up in the middle of the night, banging my head on the guard rail, okay?"

"Anything you say."

"See? Anyone could read *those* feelings. I bet if I flashed you right now, I could kill you on the spot." Joking was better than frustration, so I smiled. "We were fine at the prison, but then your little toy decided we should leave. But why did we listen? I know your reason, but what about the rest of us?" She leaned over to look in at Syd again, then straightened up and looked me in the eye. "Don't you ever wonder if we should make our own decisions, in some way more self-serving than asking your Llull's wheels to do it for us? That it might make the most sense to simply do what *makes* sense—stay put where we were comfortable, and not even pick up that thing?"

"Sometimes; almost. But then I always decide we should stay with what's worked." I felt a little defensive. "No one else ever objects, not even you."

"Exactly, and I don't even think that something is *making* us agree. It's not like that." Her left fist was shaking as if she had dice in it. "It's not that something is *doing* something. What's the opposite of that?"

"Something passive?"

"Bronze star, maybe. I've been able to figure out the simple stuff, though, like for us to do something other than just follow that machine of yours, we would have to have another idea. Simple, huh? So—and this is just as simple—something is keeping us from having that other idea. I can see that when I look at any of us. If I knew why I see it, I'd know.... But sometimes it acts, too, Alistair, I think. And when it acts it's the thing that makes me want to sing only 'The Wonderful Widow.' What the hell is it, Alistair?"

"A mystery serenading itself." I still wasn't following her very well, so instead I was trying to make her smile in return for the smile she'd given me earlier.

She shook her curls back from the sides of her face so I could see the expression in her eyes. It was eloquence itself; it certainly wasn't a smile. I had been right all along: the role of friend was much more difficult than admirer-from-a-distance.

CHAPTER FIVE

BECAUSE THERE WERE SO few of us now, we decided it was time we took the plunge into the realm of chaos theory: we let Bo take the wheels the next morning as we passed the Dearborn sign at the 94/39 split. He spun the wheels and read out, "Wichita \ Invert," and "Wall \ Reverse Yourself."

"Why would you put 'Wichita' on the wheel?" Mean Jean asked, shaking her head. It was the first time it had ever come up on a spin, but I knew Mean Jean had been waiting to complain about its inclusion. It may have been because of her military background, but Mean Jean was of all of us the most in favor of continuing to use the Llull; even more so than I. It seemed that for her, a confusing order was better than no order, may even have seemed familiar; but even she had her limits.

"Dorothy was from Kansas," Bo said, as if this settled the question. He squinted up into the sky. "We just have to watch for houses dropping down on us."

"You could say that it refers to Greenfield Village," Dully said. "Historical houses have been moved there from all over the country."

"Houses from Kansas?" Bo said.

"I can't say. But it's only a few miles north of here."

"What do you say, Bo?" I'd heard of the village, part of a conglomerate of hoardings by the Moses of Michigan manufacturing, Henry Ford. He had gathered in old machinery, vehicles, even houses, and set them off in a park, a dour industrialist's take on Disneyworld.

"Let's go see where Kansas landed," Bo said.

"In that case, I will be leaving you here," Dully said.

"Abdullah! Why?" asked Mean Jean. She sounded upset.

"I want to keep moving east; north doesn't interest me."

"That's not it," Marcella said. She stepped out from behind the lawn spreader and walked over to him. "What's your real reason? What do you know that we don't?" I didn't know what Marcella was seeing in Dully, but she wasn't about to let him go without answering her questions.

"For me, that place is the heart of American darkness, a kitschy patch over a hellhole dug by capitalism, by cruelty and greed. I'm not a jihadist—even in regard to the Oscar Meyer Wiener-mobile, I say 'Live and let live.' But to go visit there is to admire the power of Ford's money. I want no part of the worship of capitalist idols and images. I wouldn't feel clean there."

"That's an extreme position," I said.

"Yes," Dully said. "So my family told me, as they went off to ride in the Model Double-A bus past the slave plantation while they drank Ginger Beer. There's nothing real there, Marcella; it's all an illusion created by a little rat-faced man too cheap to buy a suit that fit. I wish you all every blessing, but I'll keep stubbornly going east."

"Bo read out 'Reverse Yourself,' too," Mean Jean said. "Why can't we just turn around, or spin again?"

"I want to see where Kansas fell from the sky," Bo insisted.

"Go, see. *Alla-hu Akbar*; Ford is not great for me; your Llull is not great for me, either." He smiled, "Dearborn, now, Dearborn is great—even if it's slipping toward the sink!" He waved and started walking, east along I-94.

"Abdullah!" It was Mean Jean. She stood in the center of the road. "Abdullah, take me with you?" What had begun sounding like an order had ended as a plea.

"Of course, yes; but you must come now." She grabbed one of her bags and started to run after him. "No, no, you must bring your dowry," he told her.

"My dowry?"

"I've had my eye on that inflatable pool you sleep on," Dully said.

Mean Jean turned back, bent down, and pulled the folded pool off the bottom of the popcorn wagon she had been using as her moving van. She tucked it under her arm and hurried to catch up with Dully, who had started walking and didn't look back.

And then we were four.

"Now who'll cut my hair?" Bo said. He went to the

popcorn wagon and looked inside. "She left her barber kit." He held it up.

"I'll cut your hair, Bo," Marcella said.

"That was a surprise," I said.

"The haircut or Genevieve?" Marcella said.

"Mean Jean following Dully."

"What was surprising about that?"

"Well, she talked so tough all the time, and just now she practically pleaded with him to take her along." Mean Jean was hurrying to catch up with Dully. "She looks very much the dutiful little woman. Think they'll have sex?"

"Only if he demands it," Marcella said. "But he's only her guide to Dearborn. She'll leave him soon enough." She was checking Syd's safety belt.

"What?"

"She's looking for someone a lot more basic than Dully."

"You mean a jihadist."

"No; something more fundamental than any mere religion. She wants a man who thinks a woman should be told what to do, and will make her do it, no matter if she says she wants to or not."

Amused, I looked at her dwindling figure in the distance. "I didn't think such women still existed."

"And when's the last time you asked yourself if *you* still exist, Alistair?"

"What's that supposed to mean?"

"She's just like you. She doesn't want to have the responsibility of making her own decisions. So, just to keep you happy: *Alistair, get a move on!*"

* * * * * * *

There was a large gate in the brick wall around the village, and this opened into the grounds. The museum was a huge building off to our left. The gate reminded me of the prison we had stayed in, but the prison had only been surrounded by fences and so had had a much better view. Once through the gate we tiptoed through a plaza filled with broken bottles, and found ourselves in a green space dotted with an assortment of historical and architectural curios—each structure separated and presented in a square of sidewalk, each a world-class representative of a kind of house or of a person; architectural alpha males and females. There were balloon frame and clapboard houses, the ricky-tick of Victorian porch filigree, a windmill, workshops where Edison had once paced and boasted, where Henry Ford had rolled out his long black ribbon of Model A's, where the Wright Brothers had drawn the wire for the spokes for their custom bicycle wheels. The air was filled with the sharp, heavy smell of silage. If, instead of coming here to immolate themselves, the Lems had come to gather a representative exhibit of our world's history, this place—looking so corn-fed and upright that even the peeling paint seemed a mark of Puritan restraint— could have served as *Diorama Americana*.

But there were people in this diorama. They were sitting on the porch of a white clapboard house. To my eye the house was overly symmetrical: the front door dead center under a perfectly pitched façade; the same number of windows on each side of it; two chimneys—mirror opposites of one another—on the sides; even the blocks that made up the foundation were perfect mirrors of one another. *The Noah Webster House*, read the plaque in the tall weeds. *Webster lived here when his dictionary was published.*

On the small porch sat two women and three children. A fire was burning in the center of a small square of cinder blocks just off the edge of the porch. A man came walking quickly from around the side of the house where a stack of wood showed above the stalks of the overgrown lawn.

"Hello," one of the women called out. She stood up, took a little girl by the hand and walked down to the road. "Where are you headed?" She was blonde, with a slight overbite and bangs snipped straight just over her eyebrows.

"We're not certain," I said. "A place big enough for us to settle for a while."

Bo, being Bo, said, "The Inverted Witch's House."

"Wichita," Syd said.

The woman laughed. Her little girl walked out into the road and stood staring up at Syd seated in her throne on the chrome lawn spreader.

"In that case, you'll want to turn around. You're headed the wrong way," the man said as he walked through the weeds to join us. He had a thin face and a long chin, as curved as the back of a spoon, a face that made him look sad even as he smiled at us. I noticed, too, that he kept one hand in his coat pocket; "A pistol," I thought.

"We are?" Bo said.

"Yes, the 'Inverted House' is back that way, the other side of the tracks and through the wall." He pointed toward an opening in the distance, but all I could see was a pile of red-brown bricks that had been knocked down, maybe bulldozed.

"Daniel," the woman tried to sound disapproving, but failed. "Explain yourself to these people."

Daniel only shrugged; I noticed that he still had his hand in his coat pocket.

"I'm Brenda," the woman said with a shake of her head. "Come in, come in. Come see where Noah Webster lived." Marcella and I hesitated—the house was not big enough for our small band to be comfortable in, and there was the question of whether Daniel did have a pistol—but Bo, smiling, simply followed them up the short walk. The woman and the other two children, both boys, followed Brenda inside. Marcella untied Syd from her throne and we three brought up the rear with Daniel.

The house inside was the opposite of the house outside. Where the outside had been disturbingly perfect in its bilateral symmetry, the inside was unbalanced and convoluted. Two steps inside the front door we met with a railing across our path; beyond that was a hole in the floor that looked down on a lower level where we could see an old-fashioned kitchen. To our right was a small room with rows of dark, oily-looking books on high shelves. To our left was a large airy room. Brenda led us into that room. "This way," she said, and we followed, stepping on one another's heels like dancers under a Chinese dragon. Two more rights led us back to the other side of that odd pit in the hall. From there we took a set of switchback stairs to the second floor, then another left down a hall, a right through a long narrow bedroom, and then down two small steps set cross-corner-wise, into a small room that met the bedroom at a right angle. It was like being spun around for a game of blind man's bluff. If there hadn't been windows all around I wouldn't have known in what direction I was facing.

In that small room there was a small, glass-door fireplace with a low fire and a narrow trestle table surrounded by ladder-back chairs. Brenda invited us to sit. She poured out glasses of room temperature tea, and then sat near the end of the table. Daniel sat at its head.

"Comfortable?" Daniel asked.

"I am," Bo said, but Daniel was looking at Marcella. I began to wonder if this were a polygamy recruitment station.

"Surprisingly so," Marcella said, sipping the luke-warm tea and watching the tiny fire. Syd was on the floor near her feet, intent on something the other little girl was showing her.

"Don't you wonder why?"

"Oh, Daniel," Brenda said, touching the man's arm. "Don't be so dramatic." She smiled at us. "When we came here we were like Goldilocks—trying the biggest house, trying the next smaller house; none of them were right. We figured we would probably have to just give up and live in the huge barn down at the end of the park, there being only six of us. Not enough for a small house. We only came in this one to look for pans or blankets. It was Carol Sue who noticed that the walls didn't press in on us here." She nodded toward the other woman, who had been silent the entire time. Carol Sue had dark hair; her more prominent overbite suggested that she and Brenda might be sisters. "We still need the fires sometimes—it depends on how rambunctious the boys are being, but we found we were mostly comfortable here. We couldn't figure out why, but Daniel thinks he knows, don't you Daniel?"

Daniel had clearly been waiting for Brenda to give him his cue. "It's the layout," he said. "That's why. The shape of the spaces here, their ups and downs and turns, is so odd that we never feel that we've centered ourselves in it; any time we lift our heads and look across a room into another one, it's like we're looking into an entirely different house, so we never feel confined. The rooms, halls and stairs here are as convoluted as one of Webster's word derivations." He looked very proud of having come up with this image. He watched us, clearly waiting for our reaction.

"Huh!" was Marcella's response. As I've said, she was for the most part totally immune to obligation.

Daniel's idea was actually no wilder than many of the theories I had heard over the last year and a half, and obviously something was letting the six of them buck the new psychology and live in this small house. I was impressed.

"That would never have occurred to me, even as a possibility," I said. "That's brilliant." The expression on Daniel's face told me this had been the right thing to say. He took his hand out of his pocket, laid a welder's scratch sparker on the table top, and clasped both his hands around his tea glass.

"But, I'm sorry to say," Brenda went on to say, "none of the other houses here are this convoluted."

"That's because there aren't any more dictionary writers' houses," Daniel said. "Farmers and inventors think in straight lines."

"Whatever the reason," Brenda said, touching Daniel's hand, "because there are only four of you you'll have to take one of the really big spaces, won't you? The barn is dry and it's just down the road from us. Your daughter could come over and play with ours any time."

"She's not their daughter," Bo said. "What about the inverted house? You said it was the other way."

Daniel nodded. "What you want is Buckminster Fuller's Dymaxion House. Do you know who Fuller was?" Daniel reminded me of Rich in his eagerness to explain things.

"Geodesic domes," I said. "Not straight lines."

"Short straight lines close together," Daniel said, with a lift of his spoon-like chin. "But the house came before the domes; just after World War II. Most houses are built up from the ground, but Fuller's house hangs down from the sky. The whole thing is suspended on steel cables from a central mast—and tension keeps the cables straight. The house itself doesn't touch the ground. It's smack in the middle of a big exhibition space inside the museum building, so you shouldn't feel too pressed. There's even a broken skylight to let smoke out when you build your fires."

"Come on, Marcella, let's go see it," Bo said.

"When I finish my tea, Bo."

"And there's one more thing about the house that your little girl got exactly right."

"Syd did? What's that?"

"The house originally stood in Wichita. In fact, there's a ventilator built into the top of the house—you'll see it, it looks like the crest of some tropical bird—and its purpose was to channel any Kansas tornado winds from under the house and out the top so the house wouldn't collapse on itself."

Syd, having heard her name, was looking up at Bo. "Collapse on itself," she said. Her remark was funny, but it was something else, as well.

* * * * * * *

The gigantic enclosed space of the museum was a Sargasso of equipment cast up by nearly four centuries of humans compensating for their various frailties and shortcomings, mental and physical. There was the oldest surviving steam engine, tractors that towered over our heads; there was a sign with an arrow pointing off into the dark center of the hall that read *The JFK Limousine,* but none of us even looked that way. We walked straight ahead, staying close to the perimeter of the building where light came through tall windows.

We were watching for Buckminster Fuller's name. We first found it on a sign pointing to a small exhibition space, certainly too small to hold a house, even one that hung down from the sky. We pointed our flashlights into the room and saw what looked like a fifteen-foot seedpod on three rubber wheels. *Bucky Fuller's 1934 Dymaxion Car*, a small sign read. A larger one read *[Fuller + Noguchi] the best of friends.* Arranged around the car, in transparent plastic display boxes, were sculptures made of pieces of wood suspended in tangles and spans of wire, sleek metal castings of abstract shapes, and stacks of odd chairs. In the image printer just inside the doorway there was a strip dangling: a beautiful young girl with Asian eyes in a stocking cap standing unsmiling next to one of the wire and wood sculptures.

We went inside for a closer look at the car. I pulled the door open and found it was only a shell; inside there was no engine, only a single seat and a false steering wheel. Marcella strapped Syd into the seat and we placed the biggest of our flashlights on the dashboard, pointing forward past the car's blunt nose. Then we slowly wheeled her around the exhibition space, with Bo making engine and gear-shifting noises, and out into the main hall. We made a left turn and we saw it.

The Wichita House hung centered in a rotunda-like

space all its own. A sign proclaimed,

Step into the Future!
Come Tour Bucky Fuller's "Dymaxion House."

Water and leaves, twigs and birds had all made their mark on the Dymaxion House. All around the curved body of the house the rainwater run-off had streamed to the floor, creating a green circle of mold, moss and scrawny grass, but the sides gleamed and all but one of the windows were intact. The house was circular, with a gleaming metal roof (with the tornado ventilator just as Daniel had described it), a pie-slice shaped living room some twenty-five feet across, beautiful wooden floors, paternoster shelves, and a central mast from which the house did indeed hang—it looked like the central mechanism of a merry-go-round. We walked through it, marveled at how compact it was, found a broom and swept up all the broken glass for Syd's sake, and knew we couldn't stay inside it.

We built our fire in a space surrounded by empty plinths. Directly above our heads there was a rectangular hole in the roof where there once had been glass. Three girders crossing the cloudy sky were all the remained of the skylight. The gleaming sides and roof of the Dymaxion house threw shimmering bolts of red, yellow and blue light against the walls and the intact stretches of ceiling. It was like sitting inside a kaleidoscope.

* * * * * * *

"'Where do you come from, and where are you going?'" Marcella suddenly said after we'd eaten. She was watching the firelight skittering over the still-shiny parts of the house. "'Look up, speak nicely, and don't twiddle your fingers all the time.' Do you remember who said that, Alistair?"

"Everyone's mother?"

"The Red Queen in *Alice in Wonderland*," Bo said. "I love that part."

"It's just after Alice finds that no matter how hard she tried to walk away from a house, no matter what path she took, she always ended up right back there. She says, 'I never saw such a house for getting in the way! Never!'" Marcella said. "I've never stopped asking myself why we left the race track and came here of all places. And the most important questions I've come up with are simple ones: Where did we start? Where did we go next? And why are we here now?"

"We're just moving because we feel we need to move. It doesn't mean we're in a fairy tale."

"*Alice in Wonderland* isn't a fairytale," Bo said. "It's a book, and the guy who wrote it was a mathematician."

Marcella ignored him. "You're right, Alistair, we're not in a fairy tale. Our wanderings are straight out of a cheap psychology book: sudden death and homelessness causes withdrawal—so we all holed up in a prison. And where did we go next? To a figure-8 racetrack, where we could have the illusion of getting somewhere, when we were really going nowhere. And now we've come to view the future—and what do we see? That the future never happened, and now it never will; the future is a bird-shit-stained shambles."

"There are still a few bright spots there," I said, trying to make her smile. It didn't fly. "And why are you bringing all this up now?"

"I'm not." She shook her head. "*I'm* not. And I don't know what is. That's my point."

"What do you want us to do, Marcella?" Bo asked. He looked scared again.

"I don't know what you two are going to do, but Syd and I are going on a sleepover, at the Webster house."

She packed a few things, took Syd by the hand, and they walked off toward Noah's Webster's house. It was the saddest evening I'd had since I'd left the server room; without Marcella, without Syd, the quiet was like a sweaty palm pressing down on us. Bo and I moved to opposite corners of the exhibition space and I watched the kaleidoscope all around us, spiked through by the occasional Lem, until I fell asleep.

* * * * * * *

I awoke to the music of Marcella's voice:

*Our dumb city's on a Hallucinatory Ma-ap
Ruby Buddhas are sucked off the breasts uh-of—
of of of of of of of of...*

"Good morning," she said. She was packing a pack, scattering things across a wide space as she searched for something.

"Good morning," I said.

"Where's Syd?" Bo asked. His hair was standing straight up and his eyes were bloodshot.

"I left her with Brenda, Carol Sue and Daniel."

"Left her for how long?"

"For good. She's going to live with them."

I sat up and stared at her. Bo's face went pale. "What? No; go get her back!"

"Bo, this is what I do. I take custody of damaged children until I find the right place for them."

"Her right place is with us."

"Trust me. That crooked old house is the best possible place for Syd, and those are the best possible people."

"How can you know that?" I asked her.

"Because Daniel is right. The crazy layout of that house lets them live more closely knit than anyone we've seen. And the sisters are practically clones of one another. I couldn't tell which kids belong to which sister. I don't know if the kids know, either. And Daniel is, simply, such a good man that he might have come with the house as original equipment. They'll love Syd because they know she needs it. It's that simple to them. They'll love her even if she never gives them a single smile. This is what I do, Alistair; this is my work. I've always only kept kids until I could put a roof over their heads, and, think about it, where else am I going to find a family with an actual roof *now*? I know what I'm doing.

"And besides, I can't take her where I'm going."

"You're leaving us?"

"It's a pretty small 'us' now, Bo. Just you and me and Alistair. I'm off to the sink."

"But why?"

"It's dangerous there," I said. "You're safe with us."

"Safe doesn't interest me anymore, not on these terms. Look out there," she said, pointing across the museum, through the hole in the ruined wall, where I could just make out a new group of people making camp on the grounds in front of the Edison Workshop. "It's another band of wanderers. They're setting out some food, they've got some kids running around, and the adults are already sitting by fire talking. The new face of slavery," Marcella said.

"Since when does sitting around a fire talking count as slavery?" I asked her.

"Since we haven't had any other choice; since we can't do anything else. It's been the same for every group of people we've encountered, Alistair. Haven't you noticed? We've all been sorted into little bands, our psychology adjusted so all any of us wants to do is to wander around and sit by fires together, but not really together. We've been left with just the slightest touch of sex drive, enough to give a little cohesion— although Rich, and certainly you, Alistair, may be exceptions there. No one plays cards, no one plays ball, no one looks for a real relationship, no one talks about the emotional lives we've lost....Did you know that I have, or had, children of my own, three of them? And that I don't know where they are, or even if they're still alive; that I spent three months running the streets of Adrian screaming their names like a mad woman?"

"You never told us."

"Do you even care?"

"Of course I do; we do."

"I don't doubt you, Alistair," Marcella said, touching me lightly. "But neither you nor anyone else ever asked me about my life beyond what I did for a living, and what I thought about the Lems and the cook-offs—and I never thought to ask you about the lives you've lost. Why? We've all had our ideas shuffled around until we've only got one or two interests that come to mind every night; the same puzzle pieces we keep trying to make fit. Don't you think that's odd, Alistair? And you know that they're doing the same thing out there right now." She pointed again at the distant group. "Can't you see how inhuman this is? Something...something is keeping us inside a narrow band, with no real contact possible. The most social thing we've ever done is to smash into one another with school busses—and that was such a bright spot in our lives, do you remember? That was just as true for me, sitting way up in the box.

"But Brenda and her family have somehow stayed together, and so already know each other without asking. And that's another reason Syd is better off with them. The rest of us, we're on a...social subsistence level, I guess you'd call it, left with only walking and talking of all the possible things people might do together, herded around in circles, like cattle in a holding pen."

"Herded together by what?" Bo asked. I'd forgotten he was there.

"I don't know, but it's happening. The best way to look at it is to say that we've been put together because we can help one another, that this combination of people is the right one for all of us. We're one another's locks and keys. But the more realistic way of looking would be to say that we've just been made into one-line actors, doomed to repeat our bit night after night without solving anything. And I'm different when I'm with you people. For one, I never used to go around singing a soundtrack to my life, like the world is some bad rock opera. We're being manipulated, inside and out, and I'm tired of it."

"But don't you have to ask yourself if it's you that's tired of it, or is 'it' making you say that?"

"I don't know what you are, Alistair, but you're not an insurance man, and you're not funny." She had been pinning up her hair, and she threw a hairpin at me. "And here's something else I've been thinking about ever since Todd's cook-off. He was about to say something about how the figure-8 was a symbol of his life, and he had told us how the patient who had cooked-off had been thinking about how everyone has a different threshold of pain. And people also have different thresholds of potential, too. I know: I spent years helping children trying to reach their fullest potential, so I know each of us has a limit. So what if cook-offs happen when a person lands on some deep truth, or steps up to the highest potential they have in themselves?"

Her hands were sketching big circles in the air, but I couldn't see if she was trying to make a shape, or if she was just frustrated. I picked up the hairpin she had thrown at me. It was bronze-gold, wavy along one edge, and had two soft, rounded tips. I put it in my pocket.

"And I ask myself," she went on, "are we being kept in little packs so everyone can help everyone else find that profound thought that only they might have, or because the limited subjects that come to mind help delay us getting there? Is all this pointless wandering around offensive or defensive? And I don't know, Alistair. All I know is that we seem bound to just keep wandering and talking until we've all lifted ourselves as high as we can go, then we're turned into minerals and lifted into the sky, with no choice in the matter. Sounds like slavery to me.

"And so" she said, buckling her backpack, "the world is meant to end, not with a bang *or* a whimper, but with a dull fireside chat. Hell, I'm tired of chatting. So, I'm off to the sinks—to see what I can see where the physical rules."

Then, turning her back to Bo, she lifted the hem of her jersey and flashed her breasts at me. I had just enough time to see that her nipples were the small, tight sort, like acorns viewed end-on. Through the sudden rush in my ears I heard her say, "It seems I don't have as much potential as I thought I had—you're still here. I admit it, I'm a little disappointed in myself." With that she straightened her jersey, kissed Bo on the forehead, shouldered her bag, and walked off toward the hole in the wall.

CHAPTER SIX

THAT EVENING BO AND I, both feeling a little lost, sat on opposite sides of the fire. The Dymaxion house glittered, and scattered drops of rain came through the skylight. I was eating my usual—jerky, corn chips and grated cheese, and Bo was eating his usual—caraway cocktail rye without butter, to be followed by a full pack of spearmint gum. It was a wonder either of us was still alive.

As we ate Bo made animals shapes from old coat hangers he had found—"oryx," he said, holding up a shape like a dwarf deer—and I was, as usual, half-heartedly stabbing at the pass code for the palm deputy.

"Al, do you think she was right, that something pushes us together for its own reasons?"

"I don't know, Bo; could be. Thinking is only electric pulses in the brain, so I suppose it's possible something could affect which ones fire and which ones are grounded out. But I don't think we'd ever have a way of knowing if it was." I was only half paying attention to him.

"Marcella's a smart woman, isn't she, Al?

"I always thought so, until she decided to take off

for the sink."

"So you really think that being safe is the most important thing there is."

"What? Oh, I guess I do." I'd tried so many passwords by this time, I was never sure I wasn't repeating myself. I was trying to think of words beginning with "oo," but none were coming to mind. Bo finally caught on to the fact that I wasn't paying him much attention.

"Where did you get that thing again?"

I couldn't remember what lie I'd told about where I'd found it, so I defaulted to a half truth: "I didn't just find this palm deputy, Bo. It belong to a woman I was working with. She handed it to me, then she had to leave in a hurry and didn't take it with her. And I don't know where she went."

"And if you can get that open, maybe it will tell you where she went?"

"It's possible...." Bo, with his immature and comically eccentric way of thinking wasn't likely to have a problem with how I'd come by the deputy, so I said, "The real truth is that the woman was a cook-off, and she handed this to me just before she disappeared. All I know about her is that she was an inspector for some agency trying to solve the mysteries."

"So the answer's still 'yes,' it might tell you where she went."

I laughed. "I suppose it's remotely possible, yes. But I can't get in. I've tried technical terms, names of government offices, random names—I found a baby names book in a drug store and went through page by page. At this point I'm just free associating, tapping in any word or six-character part of a word that comes to mind. Palm deputies use six character passwords. But that means there are over three hundred million possibilities."

"Three hundred million against three—you, me and the Llull. Have you asked your Llull?"

"It only gives directions."

"Then, if Marcella's theory is right, I can unlock it." He held out his hand toward me.

"Really...."

"You can't unlock it, Llull is only interested in space, and everyone else is gone. Marcella said that something put us together so our parts of thinking could help one another, but I never did anything to help anybody in our group. So, why am I here if not to unlock that thing?"

"I don't know that she meant to be that literal, Bo."

"You're smart, Alistair; Marcella is smart; Dully was really smart; your inspector probably was. But I'm not."

"You just think differently."

"That's what everybody always says. But I if do, I don't think a different kind of smart. My gift is for being simple. Please?"

I handed him the palm deputy. It was the kind thing to do, I thought. He looked at it, cocked his head, smiled, and said, "What protects a deputy?"

"Its password. You're not *that* simple, Bo. That's what we've been talking about."

"No, what protects a real deputy? A real deputy protects people, but what protects a deputy?"

Bo certainly did think differently than I did. "Well, the rule of law, I suppose. Civilization."

"Those don't fit. What else protects a deputy?"

"A gun; a car; his partner." I was beginning to feel like I was on a game show. "I don't know."

"A badge," said Bo, and he tapped in the letters. And, of course, the palm deputy sparkled into life.

I reached for it, but before he would let it go, Bo said, "Tell Marcella the last thing I said was 'I told you Marcella was smart.'"

Bo mentioning Marcella made me think—if she had been there, we both would have been giving her most of our attention. Her leaving had led to me getting into the palm deputy. What did this say about her theory?

"The last thing you said before what?"

Still smiling, Bo released his hold on the deputy. I drew it toward me. I realized as I did so that I was holding my breath.

Bo blinked and looked down at his hands, then back up at me. "I'm still here," he said; his voice was the whimper of a child. He had tears in his eyes. "Damn, damn...."

"What's wrong, Bo? You did good. You opened it when no one else could."

"But I'm still here! I'm still not good enough to disappear."

I often forgot that Bo had come to us as a failed suicide. His story of his attempt had been so comically absurd that I hadn't given any thought to how terrible must have been the impulse behind it. I couldn't find anything to say. Finally, taking a cue from Bo himself, I kept it simple: "Maybe there are more things left that only you can do."

"What else?" He was suspicious.

"The last thing the inspector said puzzled me. Maybe you can help me figure it out. She gave me the palm deputy, but she was holding a GPS, and she said to me, 'I need a compass.'"

"I can make you a compass!"

"Bo, I'm just repeating what she said."

"It'll only take a minute." He dug through one of his packs and pulled out a small leather case with a zipper. He unzipped the case, pulled something out, and held it out to me. "Hold these for a second."

It was a pair of scissors, with small square teeth along one edge. Mean Jean's thinning scissors, pinking sheers' obsessively squared cousin.

Bo next pulled out a small plastic bag. "Mean Jean was a closet scrapbooker, too" he said, and he reached over and took the scissors from my hand. He had a roll of masking tape, and he used a length of it to tape a mechanical pencil to the blade edge that was studded with small squares. The other edge he wrapped with a layer of tape. He took down one of the display cards from the curved wall behind us, flipped it over, and used his improvised compass to draw a perfect circle on its back.

"There."

And I saw that Bo was right again. The inspector hadn't wanted a directional compass, but a drawing compass. "Have you got another pencil, Bo?" As Bo rummaged through his things, I wondered why in all the time traveling with the group I had never asked for anyone's help with the deputy—and wondered why no one had volunteered. I knew what Marcella's answer would have been. Bo found a pencil.

I did what the inspector must have wanted to do: using the fliers littering the museum—*The 4-D World of Buckminster Fuller*—I correlated the cook-offs by date, time and location. The ones before the seven-month break I kept separate from those that came after. Then, using another of the thick Fuller placards and Bo's scissor compass, I tried to make a shape from this plotting. I worked on this through the evening, past Bo's bedtime, and on into the small hours, drawing and erasing, calculating arcs, my eyes scratchy, my mouth gummy. All while I was doing this some part of me was on high alert, scanning for any return of the tingling that had once seemed to me to warn of a coming cook-off.

The inspector had records of just over two hundred cook-offs with enough time and place detail that I could use them for plotting, and after no more than twenty-five of them a shape emerged: a line that the earth had intersected, then moved back out of, and then seven months later, had moved into again, not to emerge. At first the line appeared to be straight, but with a few dozen more entries my calculations told me there was a very slight but constant bowing, as if the line were an arc of an immensely long curve. When I had finished entering the other one hundred sixty-some cook-offs, the same curve remained, but the increased detail showed it to be irregular. With its pockets and ragged corners and angular bulges, it was a shape I recognized but I couldn't put a name to—until I closed my eyes and visualized it in three dimensions. The cook-offs data had sketched out the edge of a sponge, a curved sponge of immense size. The earth sinking into this invisible sponge was what was causing the cook-offs, or at least was the possibility space where they happened. As jarring as this was, it was actually only a small answer that led to bigger questions: What was it? Where had it come from? And what did it have to do with the Lems? But I couldn't stay awake any longer, and even as I worked to describe a catenary, in the middle of writing "cosh $x = \frac{1}{2} (e^x + e^{-x})$," I fell asleep.

* * * * * * *

I awoke to find Bo kicking through the clutter under the ramp that led to the door of the Dymaxion house. "I went to see Syd," he said. "But she didn't want to play with me any more. Then I went over to try to join that new group, but they wouldn't even talk to me. They just turned their backs. I guess they must already have a Bo."

"Must be."

I told him what his success with the palm deputy had shown me, and once again he proved to have thinking processes very different from my own. He said, "A sponge? Is it soaking something up or squeezing something out?"

"What?"

"Sponges do both."

"I...don't...."

"Don't worry about it," Bo said, "I'm sure you'll figure it out some time. But, hey, look what I found in one of the concession stands—root beer barrel candies." He held the roll out for my inspection. He had already eaten almost half of it.

"So, a little variety for your diet."

"I could use some. I hate spearmint gum."

"Really? If you hate it why do you chew it for dinner every day?" I sat up and opened a bottle of water to clear my throat.

"I don't know. Just a habit I picked up after my trip over the falls, for no reason—like a pregnant girl's craving, I guess."

This was a whole new mystery—before I could completely solve one others were always cropping up. I got to my feet and paced as I talked. "Organic molecules are right and left-handed, Bo. Caraway and spearmint have the same elements, but they're opposite handed.

"All life on earth is based on left-handed amino acids and right-handed sugars. The theory is that this was somehow imprinted on the molecules in interstellar space before the solar system and maybe even before the galaxy was formed. And what they think causes this is an odd kind of light, circularly polarized light. Two fields of linearly polarized light add together and this creates the rotation."

"Round light?"

"Circular polarized light."

"From outer space."

"It's here, too, Bo. Light reflected from scarab beetles is circular, left-handed light. Light reflected off some shrimp does the same thing. Fireflies give off both right and left-handed light, one from each side of their lantern. But, yes, mostly it's something that's found in interstellar space."

"So what's from outer space, my bread or my gum?"

"Neither; they're both from earth, both fine. Some other mirror molecules are dangerous, though. An old drug called thalidomide had right and left hand molecules—one molecule cured a pregnant woman's morning sickness, its mirror image deformed her baby."

"That's terrible." Bo looked like he was about to cry. "A mom and her baby on opposite sides of a...."

The glycerin splash soaked the uneaten part of Bo's caraway loaf. The hurricane relief ventilator on top of the Dymaxion house creaked through a half turn, and then was still again. After my paralyzing chill faded, I found myself hoping that somewhere Bo was happy now. But "I told you Marcella is smart" hadn't been his last words after all.

CHAPTER SEVEN

S<small>INK</small> DT, <small>LIKE MOST</small> big cities, had once been bordered by a rising terrain of small houses, stores and brick two-stories, built in uneven concentric rings. The almost over-night eradication of the middle class and the simultaneous casting adrift of NASA had changed that. Urban populations had been compacted, and the huge NASA trucks and loaders that had once moved boosters and shuttles across rocket-blackened tarmacs were sent by HUD to rip houses in crumbling neighborhoods out of the ground, move them in toward the centers and drop them onto hastily bulldozed inner city lots. So rectangular pits and sprawls of weedy land where broken and twisted pipes pointed crookedly skyward edged my approach to Sink DT. The trucks' Leviathine tires had corrugated earth and concrete alike—giant rumble strips marking the edge of the drop-off to the sink—and walking was difficult. I knew that at this range I would encounter few stragglers or individuals; nearly everyone would have been drawn, smiling and snarling, into the sink center.

There is little of the hero in me; heroism, after all, is not a passive process. But I wasn't planning any heroics: this was a topologist's mission. The plan was to find Marcella and explain to her what Bo and I had figured out, tell her what things had changed and maybe, too, what things still remained the same. What would happen next depended on her reaction. A typically passive plan.

But finding Marcella wouldn't be easy, I knew. Sink DT had steadily shrunk through the first two dozen years of the twenty-first century, but even as compactly compassed as it now was, it was still a sprawl. I knew that Marcella considered the garish corporate co-opted ballpark to be the center of the city, so that was where I planned to begin my search for her. I had had to leave my cart behind, and took only what I could carry across the broken landscape. But in addition to the pack on my back, I had brought along the Llull machine. I kept a mental picture of the bilateral symmetries of the ballpark in mind as I spun and read the wheels. Llull moved me through the ruins as aimlessly as a moth, but I felt sure I was getting closer to Marcella with every spin of "Bacon Fat," every turn of "Industrial Breakdown."

For more than three weeks I was in the sink though not of it.

When I had stopped to say goodbye to the disinterested Syd, Brenda had given me a pair of opera glasses she had found in one of Noah Webster's rooms—a small pair of jeweled binoculars on an elegant ten-inch stick. Feeling a little absurd, I used these to scan around me as I moved through and around the rubble, keeping an eye on the glintings of steel and glass, watching the pods of people passing in masses, looking in vain for a long cascade of yellow gold curls. I heard whistles and groanings like whale speech rising up out of unseen basements and out of rusting of semi-trailers, but didn't investigate. Even in a sink the Marcella I knew wouldn't be there.

The psychology of the crowds in the sink was just as Rich had described it over chicken and wine—small spaces were literally jammed with bodies of all colors and ages, some naked, some violent, some unconscious, some just limp with blissful smiles, all wriggling around one another like worms in cans; underground garages echoed with wet slaps, cries and low sexual moans. Gas fires flared everywhere, casting an ashen pall and a sour stink over the compacted, disheveled buildings, the shingles of civilization laid bare. A few children wandered around unattended, dirty and naked, but I never saw one crying. The one small girl I offered to help tried to bite me, and after that I let the entire short-people species be. They all looked to be thriving. A giant NASA truck—really not much more than huge wheels and an open rectangle thirty feet off the ground—whirred through the rubble one morning with a twenty-some-foot bronze fist slung beneath it in a net of black chains. I saw corpses lying in the open, but even these were reassuring in an odd way: a dead body in a field, its throat slashed, was a more familiar human fact, sad but understandable, than were the disappearances or the Lems. In fact, all these Boschian scenes gave me a deep homecoming feeling, settled my stomach to something like a simmer: this was exactly the post-collapse world we had all expected, a world we all knew well from shallow films and airport book rack thrillers. So the chaos was in its way comforting, like a walk through a familiar theme park, an unthreatening vacation trip to Madness Land, so much so that I forgot myself and took a long swig from the spigot of a fountain that gushed over a broken and moss-clogged pool in a triangular park.

Within minutes my kidneys felt as if they had been filled with gears, parts of some machine that was now trying to assemble itself in those bread-roll-shaped sacs, tearing loose everything there to give itself room. When I tried to think, my words appeared imprinted in my head on shiny ribbon-thin rhomboids that slithered over one another like snakes in a pit, refusing to order themselves into anything intelligible, as if the language wiring in my head had all been pulled loose and reinstalled in a series of dead shorts. In my delirium, I saw a schematic of myself lying in the rubble as if from above, saw my body as a long rectangle, my head as a small square at its end, the pillow I'd made of my coat as another rectangle under my head, all of this centered inside a giant round sponge—DaVinci's proportional man in renal meltdown—and I "knew" that until I aligned all these perfectly I would never get better. I wriggled and twisted until I accomplished all these perpendicular alignments. Then I had to turn on my left side and align everything again with the same precision. Every time I coughed I saw concentric gold rings shooting off into distant space like curved darts. How many hours I lay doing this, and trying to keep my head clear of those slithering loose words, I can't say.

At one point I opened my eyes to a vision of a beautiful short-haired girl with Asian eyes propping me up and feeding me soup out of a cup. That may have been a hallucination. In one of my fleeting lucid moments, I realized that Bo's comically eccentric personality, his odd way of thinking that had amused all of us after he joined up, his quirks that had helped me unlock some secrets, had all been a result of his trip over the falls, of having swallowed too much water—of brain damage—and that Marcella had probably recognized it, while none of the rest of us had. And in that same brief moment of clarity I knew that if I hadn't coaxed him to think about handedness he would still be around. After that I was out again.

The next time I opened my eyes they focused on a six-foot or so bungee cord lying in the dirt near an old fire site some dozen feet from where I was laying. I made it on hands and knees. I wrapped the cord around my neck and pinched one of the end hooks over the loop. It was a poor excuse for a leash, but the best I could do. I dipped my finger in the ash and wrote three words on the back of the Llull machine, hoping the shaky letters would be legible, hoping it wouldn't rain. It was after dark when I finally finished. I lay on my side to ease the stabbing in my kidneys, watched two deep green Lems burn across the sky, cried out when I let go a burning stream of urine and blood, soaking my pants, and, finally, with ribbons of words and equations swimming behind my eyes like tiny piranha chasing my optic nerves, I passed out from the pain.

CHAPTER EIGHT

"ALI–STAIR, ALI–STAIR *Ben*–jamin!" Someone was reciting my name as if it were a song. "There are probably other Marcellas here. The name was trendy, once upon a time. You could have been taken to any of them, and some of them might have eaten you alive."

I opened my eyes and saw someone standing above me, leaning over—but it wasn't my Marcella. And then it was. I'd been expecting to see her long hair in the sunlight, a pre-Raphaelite desolation angel. But what I looked up toward was a smiling, athletic sylph, a slim girl with gold blonde waves trimmed to less than a finger-length.

She wore torn jeans and a dark green T-shirt with the phrase *Ergonomics My Ass!* printed across it in white. The shirt was cut off at the bottom of her sternum, leaving her belly bare, the upcurves of her breasts just visible. Her freckles, at least, were familiar. "What were you thinking?" she said with a grin.

I propped myself up on my arms. My pants were dry, but smelled foul. "I was pretty sure you would stand out, even here," I told her.

She leaned down to finger the ash-writing on the

back of the Llull Machine. *"Property of Marcella,* huh?" She tugged the bungee cord. "And this leash thing around your neck, that's a nice touch. I notice a definite consistency in how you think of me."

"I figured if anyone who found me thought I was sick, they might just leave me to die, but if they thought I was unconscious as part of a sex game, they'd be a lot more likely to take me to you. I might not have been thinking clearly."

Marcella laughed. "In another life your kind of unclear thinking might have suited me just fine—even if you look old enough to be my pervert uncle." She shook her head; her short curls danced. "But this isn't that life. And the sex groups, so I hear, don't bother with names. I'm an outlier here, Alistair, I'm not here to be part of the groups, or the gropes, for that matter. Well, not very often, anyway." Her voice was breezy, her eyes sparkling. Her ever-present scowl was gone. She looked much happier than she had any of the days she had traveled with our band.

"I needed to talk to you."

"But we talked every night for over a year, Alistair. All those pointless fireside chats." She squatted down and put her hands under my shoulders, helped me get to my feet. "How are you feeling?"

"My stomach's still churning, and my elbows hurt—all my joints, in fact." I looked down at my dusty shoes. "My big toes in particular are throbbing."

"Sounds like gout," she said.

"It does, doesn't....Hey!" I had reached my hand up

to rub the throbbing at the base of my neck and was startled by what I felt. "Somebody cut my hair off!"

Marcella laughed. "That's one of milder things that can happen if you're stupid enough to pass out in the open here." She shook her own short curls, mock preening, beautiful in the bright sunlight against the gray rubble.

"Why the hell would they cut off my hair? And what happened to yours?"

"I'll show you in a bit. Let's let your stomach calm down first. And what did you want to talk to me about so badly that you were willing to poison yourself and wear a leash? And where's our Bo?"

"I want to tell you about a big sponge, and about right and left hand light."

* * * * * * *

A half hour later, we were walking under a long series of awnings on an old restaurant and theatre row. I was winding down, sputtering out random sponge facts just to keep Marcella's attention: "Their structure is the same inside and out. More than ninety percent of sponges can't live in fresh water." She squinted again to see the shapes of the cook-offs as I had entered them back into the palm deputy to create a 3-D graphic.

"I'm really sorry Bo is gone. I've thought about him a lot. I should have done more for him," Marcella said, and shook her head. Then she sighed, and turned to look at me. "Meanwhile, in other news, you think the world's inside a sponge we can't see. A giant sponge bigger than our solar system."

"Much bigger, if the rate of curvature remains constant."

"We're inside it but we can't see or feel it. How is that possible?"

"It's a different universe, I think, or at least a different galaxy. The shapes of both are equivalent in a lot of ways; topologically."

"Sponge-shaped."

"Yes. See, if we look at a series of galaxies, we see points scattered across 3-D space. To find out the original distribution they began with we have to use a gaussian smoothing window...."

"Alistair! I was looking for a 'yes' or a 'no.'"

"Sorry."

"Can't be helped, I suppose. You know what you know."

"All I'm trying to say is that I don't know what kind of energy it could be made of, but as far as the universe goes the sponge-shape is as common as dirt. It's the shape the whole universe has."

"So, we're being absorbed by an alternate universe."

"Absorbed? I don't know about that. Our universe has the same shape, and may even be the same size, so if they're absorbing us, we're absorbing them at the same time."

"Alistair, even a shortstop like me knows that all the science chatterers, all the space opera films and comic books always said we couldn't interact with alternate universes without inventing some crazy vehicle or falling down a black hole, or something. That we would have to travel there if we wanted to find our evil twins waiting for us in flying cars."

"I know. We never imagined one sharing ours in such a direct way. All the theories say we should pass one another like ships in a fog, never knowing the other exists, even if it lays on top of our own."

"They were wrong."

"I think they were."

Marcella frowned, then reached up and rubbed the short stubble on top of my head. "Do you think this other universe has people in it?"

"Math can't tell me that."

"But if that universe is the same shape as ours but made of odd energy, then life there might be something like us, but somehow made differently. Tell me about the thalidomide again?"

"One hand is good for the mother, the other...."

"*Run!*" Marcella shouted and she flashed away up the sidewalk, keeping close to the buildings as she ran. She had a white plastic bag tucked through one of her belt loops and it bounced wildly against her right hip as she ran. I looked back over my shoulder. There was a large crowd of men and women, all colors and sizes, all wearing dirty yellow shirts, coming into sight from around the corner of the last cross street. I began to run after her. We had only gone some twenty feet when Marcella stopped short: another group, all wearing black shirts, had begun pouring around the corner ahead of us. This was another familiar apocalyptic film scene, but not a comforting one. The day was glaringly bright and we were under the long metal overhang that held the marquee for a small theatre. Dust-caked cars, still cabled to their long-dead charging ports, lined both sides of the street. We hadn't been seen.

"Up here," Marcella whispered. She hoisted herself into a display window missing its glass, a dark space some ten feet deep and maybe twice that long. A banner at the back read SIMON TREGARTH—*NEW OPERA WORLD PREMIERE*. There were scattered props, a mannequin of a white-bearded Arthurian wizard seated on a stone bench, and plastic swords dangling on black threads. Marcella snatched up a stuffed falcon, wrapped a loose piece of curtain over her shoulder to cover her shirt and her belly and struck an immobile pose. I slid the point of one of the plastic swords inside my shirt and leaned back in frozen anguish. It was absurd; it was terrifying.

The two crowds moved toward one another between the rows of filthy cars, and when they met it was like a slow motion collision of two waves. Some struck out at those in different colored shirts, some fell to their knees and opened their mouths, some lay on the ground, some threw those wearing the other color shirts down on the ground. I saw one quick slashing, but that was the only blood. What we saw was a flood of sex, a heaving sea of it, slitherings, couplings, staggering human wheelbarrows, mouths, feet, hands, all occupied with others. There was gentleness and laughter, and there was the sort of slamming sex that is indistinguishable from rage. The flow of yellow shirts and black ones above bare thighs of many hues created strangely beautiful patterns, rippling waves of color that moved slowly through the population as the crowds wove through, knelt down, crawled on hands and knees and coupled with each other in twos and threes, in all combinations of male and female, and eddies of voyeurs emerged in short-lived loops around unseen acts. Gradually, like taffy stretching until it snaps, the two colors separated—the lying stood, the kneeling found their feet, the injured, smiling with bruised mouths and scratched faces, were helped by others, and the rippling color patterns disappeared, with the now separate black shirts and yellow ones continuing on their ways. As far as I could see there wasn't a single turncoat, no one clinging to his or her lover of five minutes before. They moved away, and except for a few strips of torn cloth the street was empty again. A smell like bleach and pencil shavings hung in the warm air.

"And what a wonderful world this *is*," said the Arthurian wizard mannequin. He levered himself up using his cane, and turned to us. "As big as this sink is, I never, uh uh, imagined I would encounter anyone I *knew*. Marcella, isn't it? And...."

"Alistair." I slid the plastic sword out of my shirt. My hands were shaking.

"Yes, yes. So, did you *enjoy* the spectacle? And, tell me, did you happen to notice when the shirts combined to create that moiré pattern? Truly amazing; as beautiful as the aurora, uh uh, borealis." He smiled. "It was like two species of birds coming together; lovely. Usually the groups aren't as well marked." He pointed to our left with his cane. "One of this long-time food desert's few supermarket warehouses is down at the end of this street, and that makes this an exceptional, uh uh, viewing area."

"This happens a lot?"

"Yes, Alistair. Quite a lot." It was Marcella who had answered me. "That's why I ran. I've been caught up in these twice already." She lowered the stuffed falcon. I was surprised to see tears on her cheeks.

"As have I, I'm happy to say," Rich said. I ignored him.

"My God. What happened?"

"Oh, you want details, do you? I see." She unwound the cloth that had covered her belly and laid it on the floor. "Let's just say that I can take down a woman as fast as any man can—and it ends up being a lot less painful all around." She wiped her tears away.

Rich looked at me and laughed his gasping laugh. "I believe you may have shocked your friend."

Marcella shrugged. "'*Sex is only love's best illusion, words are an imagination transfusion*,'" she sang. "But his imagination has probably already covered that ground, anyway." She was still assuming that my every thought of her was sexual. "It looks clear. Let's go, Alistair."

Rich touched my shoulder to get my attention. "I'm, how should I put it, 'in residence' here most every night. Please feel welcome to, uh uh, return any time, either or both of you, should the notion strike."

"We've got your address," Melissa said as she jumped down to the sidewalk. "This way," she said when we got to the next corner, and she pointed to our left.

"I've missed hearing you sing like that," I said as we hurried along the short block.

"Hmm. Well, I haven't missed singing everything out loud. I haven't done it once since I walked out of the Henry Ford. Obviously, me *with* you is not the same as me *without* you; I can feel my cornball strings being pulled again. And here we are, walking and talking about the same damn things. I thought I'd escaped this rut." But she smiled to show me she wasn't really angry. She looked up at the cross street sign, *Ophelia Avenue*. "The river's this way."

We checked carefully around every corner, but the roaming sexual herds seemed to have moved to other areas. I began to hear gulls and crows, and then the sound of waves slapping against the concrete breakwaters. We walked down a brick-paved incline and there was the river. In the bright sun it was the translucent glowing blue of water just out of a softener. Marcella led the way out onto a stubby pier, some fifteen by twenty feet of thick wooden planks stained with creosote. Old gray ropes were wound around the wooden pilings. Along one side I saw the pvc posts and fine mesh screening of a ten-foot wide enclosure that ran from just offshore to a few feet past the end of the pier, wrapped around and came back to the shore on the opposite side. It made the pier look as if it were caged.

I stopped just out onto the pier, but Marcella continued on to the end. The sun was at its highest now and it lit her hair and her new smile. She saw me watching her.

"Focus, Alistair, focus." She pulled the plastic bag out of her belt. "I have something to show you that I think you will find interesting." She reached inside the bag and pulled out a handful of something. She held it tightly in her fist while she wrapped a rubber band around the short very dark sheaf to keep it tight. Marcella held it up toward me, and I saw that it was hair. She leaned out and tossed it into the water just inside the caged area.

She beckoned me over, saying, "Remember those little toy dinosaurs that would fit in a capsule, then swell to the size of your palm when they were dropped in water? This happens just about as fast."

There was a bubbling and the hair very slowly pinwheeled in the water, as if a tiny maelstrom were forming. There were flecks of coral-colored foam at the ends of the hairs, foam that swelled to dozens of times its original size as we watched. Bits of the foam broke free and bobbed on the surface of the water as the hank of hair continued its slow motion twirl, shedding more of the coral foam with each revolution. Then something began churning the surface of the water around the coral flecks, something silvery and alive, about the size of big raindrops.

"What are those?" I asked. "I thought all the freshwater fish were dead."

"The coral spots are eggs, and those little silver guys are their dance partners." She leaned far over and watched the slow spinning in the water. "They're huge compared to our own, and they mate, grow and mature that much faster."

"Someone had eggs and sperm in their hair? That's revolting."

"Just the eggs. I used to do unannounced in-home drug testing, and I learned a few things. Hair straddles worlds, too, Alistair. It's biochemically dead but it grows; it's outside our body but still as much a part of our waste disposal system as our intestines—hair has chambers and spaces that pull things like drugs and mercury out of the body. But now it's providing a safe place, a chemically inert haven, for something small and alive to hide."

"But where did they come from?"

"I had no idea—until you showed up, Alistair. Now I think these are what settle to earth from the Lems. The sperm equivalents seem to be everywhere in the rivers and lakes—either that, or they spontaneously generate when the hair hits the water. I never see them until then."

I looked again at the slow twirl of the brown tuft, at the hyperactivity around the coral flecks. "Maybe that's why the water changed, to give them a hiding place, too. The crazies were right on the money—it's an invasion. And a disgusting one."

"No more an invasion than *your* galactic sponge, Alistair. And absolutely not disgusting. By the way, that's your hair."

"My hair! *You* cut it off?"

"Your sign did say that you're my property. And I needed to know if men's hair worked the same way women's does." She nodded. "They seem identical."

"Wait. Those creature's eggs were in my hair?"

She tilted her head toward the river. "You can see for yourself. And, I don't think they're creatures."

"Then what are they?"

"People, Alistair; just people. Let me show you something else."

She unbuttoned her jeans and slid them down her legs. She stepped out of them and stood in just her cut-off shirt and a powder blue thong. All her muscles were graceful and tight. The tattoo, I finally saw, was of a pair of symmetrically intertwined snakes climbing a staff topped by a matched pair of wings. I admit it; I hadn't expected her to be tattooed with a caduceus.

She lowered herself gently into the water, well away from the twirling sheaf of hair. The water came up just past her waist. She leaned forward until her face was almost touching the ripples she made, and she waded forward. She then sank slowly down until the water just touched her chin, and I saw her arms rising, cradling something about a foot long. She moved it using mostly the force of the water that her body pressed forward, as she slowly turned and waded back toward me.

"Get on your knees, Alistair, and look at what I have here."

I knelt down and leaned forward to see what floated

in the U's of her arms. It looked exactly like a fetus, a yellow gold body in a shimmering sac like a long soap bubble. A coral-colored star floated inside with it, attached to it by a short silver cord.

"What is it?"

"Don't you know a baby when you see one, Alistair? This one is only two weeks along. That's how fast they develop."

She turned away, took two steps, and lowered her arms to her sides. The sac and its inhabitant sank slowly out of sight. Marcella stood looking at it for a long moment, then turned and started wading back toward me.

"They're just buoyant enough to float about two feet below the surface, away from the birds. I put up the fencing to keep them from being swept away down-river."

She put her hands on the edge of the pier and lifted herself out of the water, twisted and sat on its edge, looking outward. "I have seven of them about that size, and there are a few more small ones. I'll have to make a bigger fence pretty soon."

"You're helping them grow? What are they when they're full-grown?"

Marcella looked over her shoulder at me. "They're not 'whats,' Alistair. They're people." She stood up then, and turned to face me. Her dark shirt clung to her and the sunlight made her wet body glow. "This is what I do, Alistair. Remember? I find children in danger of being abused and I protect them until I can find the right place for them to live."

"But if you're right and they float down from the Lems you don't know what these 'children' will become. You could be helping something really dangerous survive."

"I'm used to that, Alistair. And I have my own ideas about that." Her voice was light, her tone betrayed no hint of concern. She was pushing stray wet hairs back from her cheek. I reached into my pants pocket and brought out the hairpin.

"Use this," I said.

She looked at it and her eyebrows went up. When she raised her arms to pin her hair her breasts pushed against her wet shirt. She saw where I was looking.

"You want to touch them, don't you? Go ahead...."

When I didn't move she walked over to me, reached out, and pinched my nipples, hard. I flinched, and she laughed. "Just because I don't like crowds doesn't mean I don't like sex, Alistair." She turned away, found her jeans and pulled them back on.

The sight of her made me so happy that I had to try to take her down a few pegs—the most basic male defense mechanism.

"A strong, independent woman finding true fulfillment through the birth experience. Kind of clichéd, wouldn't you say?"

She whirled around, squared off as if she were about to strike me. I had forgotten about the children she had lost; stupid and cruel of me.

"I'm sorry," was all I could say.

"Say anything you want, think anything you want.

No one is going to harm them." She moved in close again; her scowl was back. "All the while I was standing frozen in that theatre window watching those groups of people screw their way through one another I was thinking about what you said, and do you know what I decided? I decided that this is all a swap. I think the cook-offs from here are taken away and become the Lems of that other universe you think we've moved into."

"You 'decided'?"

"Yes, I *decided*. Do you really believe we have to know everything that's happening now to go on with our lives, you arrogant jackass? Do you think sitting around more fires just talking is going to get the world rebuilt? If we're sliding in and through another exis- tence, why shouldn't there be things we don't under- stand? These children are coming in from a world with different rules. So, yes, I think all we can do is to decide to do what we know how to do and not tie ourselves up in knots over what we don't know.

"And, Alistair, I've also *decided* that our people cook-off and rain down in that other world we can't see, that other universe, and that maybe they're trying just as hard to be born there as these river babies are trying here. What were you calling that—'mirror symmetry'? Maybe this way is normal there, maybe everyone is born in bright blue water, and maybe our Lems are being born inside their bodies—and if so how much more terrified they must be than we are. I don't know if that's what's happening, but I would want someone there to be brave enough to take care of bringing those children into that world—however they might fit or might not—just like, just like, Alistair, I'm going to take care of these. Do you understand me?" She was shaking her fists. "So I don't care how these babies are different, and I don't want the others to care either. I just want the children on both sides of the swap to live. Because otherwise, both sides die. If they become a problem later, we'll deal with it, and maybe we won't even have a place in their world, but I'm used to that, too. Because this is what I do! So you can either decide to help me do this or you can decide to drag your pasty coward's ass off this pier and get the hell out of my way. Or do I need to throw you off?"

I wondered if she was right, if someone could define and shape a world just by deciding something and sticking to it no matter the consequences. With the rubble behind me, out of sight, I put the sink out of mind. I looked off across the bright river, at the sky where I knew Lems were burning even if I couldn't see them, and I looked down in the water where the tiny tangle of my hair had now sunk out of sight. This was our world now. Some things were familiar, some things were brand new: sunlight, sky and bright river, strings of proteins from another space, fired and quenched by their encounters with our atmosphere and water—in many ways conditions identical with those of the first days of life the last time around. And, I asked myself, hadn't I been trained to seek out and work with what remained constant when shapes changed drastically?

Isn't this, after all, *what I do*?

I decided to stay.

* * * * * * *

And so our days pass. Watching the long bubbles grow longer in the water, building shelters on the bricks that lead to the pier, with me hauling duct work out of the sink to create some kind of a wood-fired heater as the days grow shorter and cooler. Snow on its way. We gather food, and occasionally even have lunch with Rich. I write these notes in case whoever is born out of the water cradle we're tending should learn to read. Marcella has a milk crate full of small stones and a softball bat. Any time any of the locals heads our way, she tosses a rock in the air, and sends it, in an unerring long arc, to sting them and drive them away. Many of them know us now, and they call back, "Aw, Marcella. We're not cannibals!" But they laugh and don't come any closer.

We spend clear nights watching Lems, comfortably wound together on a luxury mattress neither of us could ever have afforded in the earlier world. But that's a world we rarely think about now. Maybe it's another effect of the new psychology, but the rational, scientific, "civilized" world we had lived in now seems to have only been a blip, a sidetrack of chance and happenstance, where people followed bright, shiny baubles of knowledge with no real goals in mind, just a Llull within the greater compass of what the world— and all its invisible twins—has always been about.

And, best of all, there's Marcella's singing:

If buttercups buzz'd after the bee,
If boats were on land, churches on sea,
If ponies rode men and if grass ate the cows,
And cats should be chased into holes by the mouse,
If the mamas sold their babies
To the gypsies for half a crown;
If summer were spring and the other way round,
Then all the world would be upside down.

That one always makes me smile.

As for my Llull Machine, I sailed it out over the river beyond the fencing, where I watched it turn through a single right-handed spin, tip and sink out of sight. I decided it was time.

ABOUT THE AUTHOR

W. C. BAMBERGER is the author, editor or translator of more than a dozen previous books. His most recent publication is a translation, *Two Draft Essays from 1918* by Gershom Scholem. His most recent novel is *On the Backstretch* (2009). Since 1984 he has been editor and publisher of Bamberger Books, based in Michigan. *A Llull in the Compass* is his first science fiction title.

www.ingramcontent.com/pod-product-compliance
Lightning Source LLC
Chambersburg PA
CBHW050408260626
47156CB00003B/927

ACADEMENTIA

In the not-so-distant future, America has been subjugated by the fanatical followers of Dr. Theo Fell, who have instituted a fascist religious regime that stifles all dissent and monitors all expression.

But all regimes have their breaking points, both personally and generally, and the Fellian States of America are no exception. The nameless narrator of this terrifying tale descends into paranoia and despair even as he rises rapidly through the academic ranks of the California Saints University system. One by one, his enemies are mysteriously overcome, until all that's left is facing the ultimate—the final—challenge: confronting Dr. Fell himself!

Borgo Press Books by ROBERT REGINALD

ACADEMENTIA

A FUTURE DYSTOPIA

ROBERT REGINALD

THE BORGO PRESS

MMXI

ACADEMENTIA

FIRST EDITION

Published by Wildside Press LLC

www.wildsidebooks.com

DEDICATION

For William

(You know who you are!)

and

For Mary,

Who was (and is) there through
Both the light days—and the dark.
Bless you, my dear.

CONTENTS

FYTTE THE FIRST

I was drifting in my pool one day,
During the merry, merry month of May,
When there came a-floating by,
The corpus of a dead fly,
Dead Fly.

Thursday, October 25th

They came for Parrott this morning.

I was grading papers in my office, when I heard the stairwell doors at the far end clang open, and two sets of iron-souled boots come tramp-tramp-tramping down our hallowed hall. I held my breath, sitting very straight upright in my chair, straining to listen, straining to pass that small turd I call my courage, until they stopped just short of my cubbyhole.

What a relief, Chief!

Then I recognized the sonorous voice of Herr Wickhizer, the Senate Sergeant-at-Arms.

"Dr. Parrott," he said, "You are accused of violating FSD #13-013. Come with us, please."

As if he had a choice. Alas, poor Parrott, I knew him, Harminius.

Let us bow our heads in silence, my dear dead friends, while I say a few words on behalf of the dully departed:

> Yea, brethren, he was a good man, a wholesome man, but not a particularly bright man, for he spoke in tongues too terribly tinged with truth.

Then I heard something I couldn't quite make out, a brief protestosterone to a scuffle, and the idiot's head suddenly came poking through my chamber door. Squawk!

"Call my wife!" he burped. "Please let her know what's happened."

Shitty-shit-shit!

I grunted no response while his arms were being locked firmly behind his back, while they marched him away, struggling, shaking, like a bug wriggling on a rusty fishhook. Caleb, Provost Security's 600-pound gorilla, made sure that *I* saw that *he* saw.

Bastard. Coward. Parrot.

We're all cowards here, so don't look too closely in the mirror, Pierre. You'll see your own eyes staring out, watching, watching, always watching.

I didn't phone poor Parrott's wife, of course. Everyone knows the campus lines are bugged.

Snug as a bug in a jug.

Friday, October 26<u>th</u>

Sometime last night the greasy gremlins came and cleaned out Parrott's office. His door was cracked just a hair this morning, and I couldn't resist a piquant peek (after quickly checking the hall for shadows). His furniture was still there—desk, chair, filing cabinet, shelves—but the family pictures, the papers, the books, anything personal, were all gone. There was a faded spot on the bulletin board outside his door where his plaque had hung.

All that's left now is his name in the few printed copies of the *Catalogue*, and that'll be gone next year, along with twenty or thirty others.

It's all very strange, Grange. A day later and a dollar short, and I find myself struggling even to remember what he looked like. I wonder if I'll demonstrate a similar lack of presence when I'm "absent."

They haven't yet asked me to pick up any of his classes; I expect they'll bring in one of the deacons again—those cheap, compliant, oh-so-well-indoctrinated bastards.

Screw 'em, screw 'em all.

Monday, October 29<u>th</u>

I was teaching Comp 101 this morning when some Amfavale stooge tried to trip me up again. I get one of these bums every week or so. We'll be talking about the use of language in Dickens or reviewing a

seventeenth-century British poet, and then some ass-hole will pop out with:

> "Well, I don't really see the relevance of this to Dr. Fell's writings,"

or,

> "How does Mr. J. Milton's depiction of Satan conform to modern Fellosophy?"

or,

> "Why did Mr. C. Dickens mock the God-manifest power of the Fellian State?"

Then I'll hem and phlegm and paw and claw, and try to say something that won't get me locked away forever.

Everything's tucked away deep inside, oh my brothers. Now I slay me down to sleep. Someone somewhere somehow must write something about everything that's anything. The funny thing is, if anyone ever actually *reads* this shit, I'm dead, Fred.

Dead, dad, dead.

Red and dead in bed.

Dead and buried.

Eradicated. Obliterated. Eviscerated. Consanguinated.

All those funny little words that mean:

"THE END OF ALL THINGS ACCORDING TO ME."

Zippydeefuckindoodaw!
No one cares, no one shares, no one prepares.
Well, almost no one.

Tuesday, November 1st

Oh frabjous joy! Oh fractious ploy! We had our monthly faculty meeting this morning. At nine o'clock we promptly filed into the courtroom, and at 9:07 A.M, promptly late as usual, Provost took his spot at the head of the room, and banged his gavel down to begin the proceedings.

"Let us open with a prayer," he intoned in his reedy little voice.

And I prayed, oh yes, brethren, I really prayed, I prayed that this cup would pass from me, preferably real soon. As usual, god or mammon or whatever wasn't much listening—at least to me.

"We have a number of important matters to consider this morning," he continued.

Oh yes, but never the ones that really matter.

I dozed in and out of three hours of announcements and discussions and pronouncements and percussions, and finally spotted the one little pertinent item buried in all this truly impressive verbiage, that *Mr. Deacon Pratt* would soon be joining the School of Arts and Theology on a temporary basis to assist the teaching of several sections of freshman comp, and would we please, ladies and gentlemen, froggies and toadies all,

welcome him, embrace him, consume him, he who is crouching over there in the corner like some long-legged spider waiting to pounce, a Leaguie bug if I ever grokked one.

No mention of Parrott, of course. He never existed.

Wednesday, November 2nd

I've been thinking too much about all this shit, and I can only reach towards the edges of answers, the crumbling flakes of my shaky life. This is a much more dangerous, damnable, depauperate, and wholly out of character thing that I've done than any I've done before. Kind of like when I was a kid, masturbating beneath the covers at night, hoping that no one would hear the heavy breathing or see the stains on the sheets next morning. Instead, here I am twanging my thing out on disk. One of these days I'll twang it once too hard and it'll fall off, along with all the rest of me.

Maybe I just don't want to go quietly into the dark. Then again, maybe I do.

Half the people I know are "Disappeared."

Thursday, November 3rd

Madame Parrott showed up at my apporchment this morning just as I was leaving for work.

"What d'ya want?" I growled in my best-of-the-mornin'-to-ya, there-ain't-no-coffee-anymore voice.

She started crying.

"Russ didn't come home the other night, and n-no

one will tell me anything about him. You were his best friend," she said, as if that really meant something these days.

Yeah, well, maybe I was and maybe I wasn't, but I sure as hell wasn't *her* friend, she who played the impeccably-coifed, stab-anyone-in-the-back faculty wife.

I wanted to shake her, to say: "You helped them, bitchess. What do you expect *me* to do!"

But she grabbed my arm, crushed her pulpy face into mine, and sputtered, "Please. Oh, please."

What could I do?

So I told her the truth, which was the worst thing that I could have done. I told her that Parrott had cracked a couple of really funny jokes about some really unfunny people at some really wrong places at some really wrong times, and that these folks really didn't appreciate his remarks really well, and now he was really gone, and you'll really never see him again, in either of our probably really short lives.

I thought she took it surprisingly well. She slapped me—once, twice, thrice. I let her, of course. Then I had enough guts left to tell her the Real Truth (which is as true as true can get, my friends):

"No one can really help you."

I left to ejaculate my little spurts of wisdom into the unlettered brains of the louts we now call studiants.

Friday, November 4th

Another week gone. I count the ways, I number the days, I'm still alive.

I've hollowed out the bottom of my soul, and poured my life down the drain of my sole. Actually, what I've done is to drill out the heel of my shoe. I put the minidisk there each night, solidly packed like a bottle of beer in an ice chest. God, what I wouldn't give for just one cold brew. *XX* or *XXX* or even a tall C'rona.

Why do I keep tormenting myself with these things? Answer my prayer, oh Grateful One, and I'll be yours forever. At least that's what I told my wife once.

I've devised a little program to wipe the 'puter clean after each session, with an extra subroutine so they can't count the keys. One of the shiny red Custodians almost walked in on me yesterday afternoon, so this morning I added a command that automatically crashes and wipes the hard drive on the verbal prompt, *shitfuckcunt*. It's not perfect, but I figure it'll shock the hell out of the good deacons, at least long enough to give the thing time to do its job.

Later, I had second thoughts and changed the wording. No point in giving them an open excuse for radication.

Fuckshitcunt.

I may be crazy, but I'm not *that* crazy.

Cuntshitfuck.

Well, not toadally, anyway.

Monday, November 7<u>th</u>

God probably had nothing to do with it, unless he had a really warped sense of humor (which he does, having created Man), but Saturday was the anniversary of the mess that started this mess. I speak, oh Great Theosophallus, of that last big bonfire of the vanities where we so carefully stuck the knife into the belly of the body politic, twisted it, and now must live with the consequences of severe political indigestion.

Funny thing was, nobody thought much about it at the time. With every election people seemed to get madder and madder, eager to point fingers at the politicians, ready to blame everything and everyone but themselves for their troubles. The Dems and Gops, they had each tried their hand at fixing things, and nothing seemed to be working, so one of the Gops denounced his own party, said it had broken faith with God (now, that's a laugh!), and organized the League.

No one really thought that his answers actually were "The Answers," but he had all the TV time that money could buy, and he convinced enough of the flock to baa-baa-black sheep in his direction that he got himself and his bunch of kooky-cutters elected.

Good ole Doctor Theo Ctistus Fell. He sure enough Fell upon us all, now that's a fact, and then he had us for lunch, with salad dressing on the side.

It was God's work, all right! See, I *told* you he had a sense of humor.

What came afterwards was the work of no god I've ever seen.

Tuesday, November 8th

Election day.

I voted, of course. So did everyone else. We all experienced together another glorious benefit of the Greater Fellian Revolution, the Univote Act, which took effect today, and which requires everyone to present their Natcit Card at their local polling station—or tell the reason why. The data are immediately transmitted to the Natcitregs for verification, identification, and tabulation. Not only does this neat little device prevent any possible voting fraud, it also ensures that every vote is cross-checked for accuracy and completeness and sanctity.

The national results were posted within a few minutes of closing time. *Mirabile dictu!*, the Amfavale coalition carried everything in sight. Great Gop warps in mysterious ways.

There were no state or local elections, of course.

Later

My "ex" called this afternoon, which immediately made me suspicious: after all, I'd shat the last deposit right on time. Of course, we didn't part on the most amicable of terms. There's nothing wrong with my "ex" except that she hasn't read a book since the age of fifteen. And that other thing, oh yes. Her laugh is a cross between a hyena's and a mule's, with a little Tarzan of the Apes thrown in for good measure. The former I could abide, so long as I had my books to

caress late at night, but that cackle, well, it just finally got to me.

We were making love one summer afternoon, and I was hump-hump-humping away, a hump-dy-dump, watching her head roll back in ecstasy or whatever, mouth open and gasping for breath, face covered with sweat, her long hair splaying nor'east and 'west of the pillow, like a pair of long pointy ears, and suddenly, oh god, suddenly out of the back of my mind came this thought. I tried to stop it, I swear to Jesus I did, I really tried, but it just kept coming and coming, like a fast freight roaring down those tracks, its headlight shining way up ahead, illuminating the words in 224-point type on the billboard rising straight before us, coming, coming, coming right about right now:

YOU FINALLY GOT YOURSELF—
A PIECE OF ASS!

Well, folks, I giggled. Couldn't help myself. Then I chuckled. Oh shit, here it comes, I thought, Hurricane Felice. I laughed, just once. She looked at me oh so strangely. Then I *HOWLED!*, oh Jesus, and I couldn't stop, after all those years of listening to her braying, I just couldn't stop. For thirty minutes, every time I'd look at her, I'd start cackling again.

Well, that was the end of our marriage, and I never saw Felice again.

So there isn't a lot to rebuild anything on, because, to tell the truth, I don't think I can ever make it with her again without busting my guts open. Anyway, it

turns out all she wanted was the phone number of a "mutual friend." As if we had any.

False alarm.

Again.

Ha ha.

Ho ho.

Hee hee.

FYTTE THE SECOND

Little critter, says I,
What wonders did you spy,
During your brief life
Of turbulence and strife;
What political maneuvers,
What window slats and louvers,
Did you beat your little brains
Against? What joys and pains
Did you decry, dead fly,
Dead Fly?

Wednesday, November 9th

Provost called me into his office this morning to discuss my "moral progress." I think he rather regards me as a toad examines a fly: for caloric content.

I was ushered into his richly endowed quarters by his equally endowed advocator, Miss Jonas, and directed to a stark, unpadded wood chair planted right in front of a huge executive desk. The latter was completely empty save for this humongous nameplate, a little something to let the *hoi polloi* know that THIS WAS ONE IMPORTANT PRICK. I have always distrusted antiseptically clean

desks and those antiseptically clean *TWOIP*s who sit behind them.

Provost leaned his auroral, amoral head back against his alligator chair, the fluorescent light radiating off the 5,000-foot crest of Mt. Crome Dome, and tried to focus on me through his tiny bifocals.

"Dr., uh...," he prompted.

I stupidly gave him my name, as if he didn't already know.

"Oh yes," he said, "very good to see you again."

He curled his lips upward in an imitation of a grin.

(Parrott used to call Bork "Dr. Burp," and solemnly intone, "Burp's up," whenever Provost walked down the hall.)

He coughed again, trying to catch his breath.

"And how are things in the English Department these days?" he managed.

Oh, they go swimmingly, you turd!

"Fine," I replied in a very even tone, "We're all doing just fine."

Fine fine fine fine fine.

"Well," he said, "I certainly enjoy these little opportunities to interface with the faculty and to discuss the things that really matter to us all."

He pulled a file folder out of his upper desk drawer, and spread it out in front of him.

"Yes, I see that you were one of the last individuals to talk to our late lamented colleague. Correct?"

He suddenly removed his glasses and looked straight at me, pinning me to my stiff chair.

"Correct!?" he continued.

"Uh, uh, uh."

I couldn't seem to think of anything to say but I had to say something.

"You mean Dr...?"

"You know very well whom I mean," he interrupted, "And I know you know very well whom I mean. And you know I know you know very well whom I mean."

I was getting lost in his syntax, with gun and camera, and I suddenly wanted to be anywhere else but Provost's office.

"He, ummm, he w-wanted me to t-tell his wife s-something," I stammered.

"And what was that?" Provost asked.

"Well, I just don't know," I replied. "Maybe to inform her about his predicament."

I thought I handled that one with sufficient ambiguity to qualify for the Theo Fell Prize in Moral Literature.

He smiled again, and I saw nothing but teeth showing behind that crocodile grin.

"And did you tell her anything?" he inquired.

"Of course not!" I shouted, much, much too fast.

Oh God, he knows, he knows, *he knows! Shitfuckcunt.* I almost lost it then, I really did, my friends, I just about spewed my guts all over that polished checkered floor.

After a minute, he replied: "No, of course not."

Then he very quietly, very deliberately, very slowly shut the folder. He very carefully picked it up with his very carefully manicured nails and put it very carefully away. He just sat there for a while picking at his

nails, sticking them in his mouth, then picking again. Pick pick pick, workin' on that railroad all the livelong day. He probably rehearses these things in a mirror.

"Dr., uh....," he finally spoke.

I repeated my name.

"Yes," he said. "Yes, yes, yes. We, that is, all of us, have been watching you so very carefully, Doctor. And we have decided that you are now ready for a further repose of trust from the California Saints University System. I therefore am prepared to offer you the position of Vice Provost for Academic Personnel, a post which has recently and regrettably become vacant with the transfer of the previous occupant of that chair to another assignment"—*in hell, no doubt*—"You would start your duties immediately, and would receive, of course, all the usual emoluments attendant upon this position. Fell's good and gracious servants must, of course, be suitably rewarded for their labor in the vineyards.

"Are you prepared to accept this assignment?"

I almost laughed out loud, the terror and the relief were so great, then had to button my lip *superdamnquick*. Bork had taken the old mounting pin, all right, and thrust it right down through my breast into the board, leaving me there wriggling and wobbling and quivering.

Damned if I did, damned if I didn't, oh my.

"Yes," I replied. "Oh, yes indeed."

Shitfuckcunt.

Thursday, November 10<u>th</u>

I keep wondering whether this is some kind of new trick, one last chance to fatten the fella up for that great, greasy slaughterhouse. They sure enough gave me a scare right from the git-go.

When I went down to my cubicle this morning, I found a couple of beefy types perched right in front of my door. As I approached, they swiveled in unison, like a pair of puffed-up kewpie dolls, and I almost turned around and ran the other way.

Then one of them grunted: "Here...to...move... furniture," or some such thing, and the beat of my heart gradually returned to a normal level again.

I take life far too seriously. I'm just a coward, Howard.

Later

My late parents, bless their rigidly unimaginative middle-class souls, would probably have rejoiced to see their eldest son suddenly made Administrative Man, not quite the stereotypical superhero, but still a BMOC. During their respectable, mundane lives they tried their hardest to ignore my not-quite-bestselling academic masterpieces, such imperishable classics of pedantic prose as *Lords Temporary and Lords Permanent*, *The Works of Robert Reginaud*, *East Is East and West Is Best*, *Katy-Did and John-Donne*, and several other equally turgid tomes, none of which they ever

understood or thought important or even bothered to read.

Did I, says I, dead fly?

Sometimes, in their ever-awkward silences, the pauses that never seemed to refresh, they almost appeared to be wondering whether I'd been left on their doorstep by the fairies—the mythical ones—or whether a teaching and writing career was really a fit occupation for a fully-grown gentleman.

Sorry, folks.

Sorry.

So goddam sorry.

> *Oh, craven old world,*
> *That has such people in't.*

Friday, November 11<u>th</u>

Provost isn't in today.

But here I am, I am, oh, quite content, if not quite spent, sitting in this fancy new chair in this fancy new office of mine, with lots and lots of space, dear Ace, plus a real wood desk, yes, and padded chairs and padded walls and padded halls; but I'm so damned scared of doing something wrong that I just sit on my padded throne and stare out the padded window. My 'puter screen stares right back at me with its unblinking yellow eye, winking at my protestations of ordinariness.

It's Cosmo the Clown, you see: he sees all, hears all, knows all. Maybe if I'm quiet they'll ignore me and go

away. Maybe if I'm quiet, *I'll* slither quietly away.
  Maybe.

FYTTE THE THIRD

A whispy voice did soon reply:
As you are, so once was I,
Full of vim, full of life,
No one's girl, no man's wife,
But the dominatrix supreme
Astride three jolly men I deem
Mine. And tomorrow I dream
Of much greater things, oh,
Of much, much *greater things,*
Of machinations and strings,
A veep's sash upon my breast;
Only then, yes, will I rest!
Dead Fly, Dead Fly.

Monday, November 14<u>th</u>

Another thrilling day in paradise.

Herr Bork-Who's-Worse-Than-His-Bite promptly paid me a visit at eight, probably to see if I was really here yet.

We must never be late, no, never late, no, never ever late!

"Well," he said, "It is good to see you finally settled

in."

He picked up a picture from the corner of my desk. "Yours?" he asked.

All mine, all mine, I acknowledged, once upon that dreadful time, and for just a thin dime, Dr. B., I will tell thee anything you want to know, and spill every bean I ever ate, and never again, never again be late.

The handsome lad there, that's Adam, Madam, drafted into the Saints Brigade some four years ago during his junior year at Gonzaga, not long before they sanctified that school; and later misguidedly shipped south to México to civilize that equally misguided country, and like Der Bingle, never being heard from again.

And the other, brother, well's she's my daughter Lou, my lovely little girl, Earl, missing these three years in the latest rendition of the L.A. riots, gone, gone, but not forgotten.

My line cometh to the proverbial dead end, it petereth out. And I would give almost all that I am to have them restored, to reset that clock back to those happy days when crime was sublime and fog was smog, when I still had a family of sorts.

"Very nice," he said.

I wanted to kill the bastard then, I wanted to scream, "You fuck, you're part of it, you murder good people in the name of God and Fell, and only the latter has anything to do with it." But I just mumbled, tumbled something inappropriate, all the while feeling like I had swallowed a giant turd. Turd from the son.

"But down to business...," he continued.

It occurred to me then that he had no emotional connection to anything real, and that I still did. I still loved my kids. I still cared. I was so surprised at myself that I missed a few of his overly precious words.

"...-cation needs to be planned very carefully. As you know, we have a...."

I just kept nodding my head and grunting every so often, like I was sitting on the shitter, and doing all these earnest things with my face. But inside me the world had shifted suddenly.

Just slightly.

Just enough.

He left me then in peace.

Tuesday, November 15th

I live, you live, he lives.

If I say the words often enough maybe I'll start believing them. I came to my office this morning feeling better than I had in months. The beast was still there, still growling inside, but muted somehow, or maybe I was just ready to let it out of its cage. There's a tremendous exhilaration in loosening all restraint.

I found a strange woman seated at the desk in the outside vestibule of my office. Her name was Smythe, Grace Smythe, and she was my new advocator. Apparently, *her* predecessor had gone the way of *my* predecessor.

She wasn't exactly pretty, what I could see of her beneath that formless gray, all-encompassing smock,

but she had this curious way of cocking her head to one side that I found mildly amusing, and she smiled ever so slightly when she spoke, one side of her mouth curling just a bit.

I decided I liked it. A lot.

She has to be a spy, Cy!

Wednesday, November 16th

I've been told to prepare an outline for Provost's talk at Monday's convocation. I try to put some notes on the 'puter, but it all turns to mush in my mind.

What am I trying to say?

Why am I trying to say it?

How now, brown cow?

Who's on first?

I have no answers to such questions, but even these circumnegations don't satisfy me anymore.

I do begin to have bloody thoughts, Botts.

Thursday, November 17th

I keep working on "The Speech," but nothing will come together. I've certainly listened to enough of this shit to be able to excrete reams of it on command. My head pounds.

Grace suddenly offers me a cup of herbal *chai* without asking me why. I know she is a spy.

Dead Fly, Dead Fly.

Friday, November 18th

Finally, finally I've got something down on paper. It's pure shit, 99 and 44/100% unadulterated excrement, so I know Provost will love it.

I leave it at Bork's office before I stagger out the door. I'm tired, but I can't sleep.

Can't rest.

Ever again.

Amo, amas, amat.

Monday, November 21st

Convocation Day.

Provost flashes by before I can catch him. I don't know whether to run screaming from the room or just to rise up and righteously confess my sins. Maybe they'll execute me for good behavior. My boring colleagues feign utter boredom.

He's using my speech!

Oh blessed relief. Oh blessed, blessed bullshittiness. It goeth something like this:

> Followers of Fell, fellow foragers on the interdemic highway of holiness, we gather together once more to concelebrate the accomplishments of ours and yours, and to acknowledge the failures of ours and yours, perpetrated and perpetuated before the all-seeing Eye of Fell.

During the past year we have made progress highly significant in radicating enemies of Fell from within and without our ranks, but much there is yet to accomplish. His studiants require the wisdom and the guidance perpetual that only we can provide unto them. His Versity and His locality require the vision sternest that only we can provide unto them. His collegialities require the vigilance eternal that only we can provide unto them. His radicators require the inspiration divine to keep all of us and them purest pure and sinless.

The California Saints University, it was coagulated on the premise that all deserving sons of God must have the obligation and opportunity to be sanctified, to save their mortal souls from the clutches of Satan and his dems. Let all libs burn forever in Hell. The gops shall inherit the earth, they shall be fruitful, they shall multiply and divide.

But still we find perversion and sin leaching from within our own ranks. The devil's tool is long and thin, and man's will is weakened by woman's wiles. Vigilant must we ever be! Purging we must continue the liberalments from ourselves and themselves. Only then can all achieve any true Fellvana.

Fell's plans this annum wax eternal, His goals fax simple and direct: we must continue down the straight, the narrow path of

self-righteousness, we must continue to fight His fight unto the very end of us all, we must continue to radicate His enemies.

And now we bless several of our newest warriors who have taken up the sword on His behalf, whom I shall introduce to the assembled Fellians of America.

The first we note is Dr. Dell D. O'Dell, Vicepro for Security and Sanctification, who promises, he says, a truly rad effort to crush freespee.

Dr. O'Dell, please rise and be counted....

The rest of the introductions rambled on in this fashion for another hour, displaying the several new members of administration and faculty, including *moi*. When finally I stood in my place, I was startled to note that none of my colleagues would eye me directly.

But I knew, oh my brothers, yes I did, I knew they were still watching me in one fashion or another. All of them, each and every one.

Dem bones, dem bones, gotta roll dem bones.

Snake eyes!

Tuesday, November 22ⁿᵈ

Provost called me to his office this morning, where he told me that he had mentioned my name favorably to Chancel last evening, as an example of how the older faculty could adapt successfully to the new Fellian ways. I shouldn't have been so pleased.

Today is the anniversary of Saint J.F.K.'s descent into Hades. I remember sitting in *kindergartendrech* when the principal turned on the radio school-wide. Even at that terribly young age I knew that something utterly terrible had just entered my terrible world, and I remember wondering how terrible it would be. That was a lifetime ago.

Grace displayed a dark green dress today, a growing, glowing green gown with plunging neckline, with rising hemline.

Oh, green grow the rushes, oh!

Shall I say Grace, Grace, and stoop to conquer?

Wednesday, November 23ʳᵈ

My first elucidation.

One Doc Ellison, Kiwi A. Ellison, accused of femtends and radthoughts. Eyes like a frightened deer's. All clothed in down, brown. Soft little shiny nose, rose. No rad mad this, Chad.

"Dr. Ellison," I began. "Why...?"

She started crying, soundlessly, tears running down the crevasses that in earlier years would have been neatly filled with makeup, so many lines etched upon the map of life.

I rattled my papers and started again.

"Subpro Clärshayt indicates that you commended the works of A. Behn to your studiants."

Radwrite. Radright.

Ellison straightened in her chair. The tears were faint contrails now, the eyes still rose, Mose. She cleared her

throat with obvious effort.

"With respect, Vicepro, I mumble-fumbled, misunderstood. Behn's work was mentioned, intention not howsomever any misguidance of innocent millicents into non-Fellian pelicans, but otherwise the contrary. Free-spee was *verboten*, misguided I am not, I grok Fellosophy. For misintention any, I crave forgiveness."

She deliberately used the jargon of a devoted Fellophile, and I found myself wondering whether this overslavishness to cant bespoke a certain measure of cynical con-Fellticantism. Not that it mattered a whitney. If I overturned Subpro's recommendation, my own position, yet none-too-sure, would quickly become none-too-few. I smiled at her with all the reassurance that I could put into my eyes.

"I believe you," I said, stamping her file "RADICATE."
And I did, too.

> *She is woman, and therefore may be woo'd,*
> *I am man, and therefore may be lewd.*

Thursday, November 25th

Thanksgiving Day.

It's the only one of the old holidays concelebrated in the Fellian States of America, unless one counts New Year's. Now that I'm a member of the administration, I have to work today, but classes are officially suspended, and most of the staff is away.

I wonder what Grace is doing: I know nothing of

her family or her personal situation. I really must remember to pull her file and find out.

Ah, how things have changed in the last few years. It was just two Thanksgivings ago that I drove into the mountains with picnic basket and friend, and had what may have been the final carefree day of my life. Fellians had begun frowning on such unescorted trips even then, but none of the socie laws had yet gone into effect, and I still naively believed things would soon turn around. They didn't.

But the sun shone brightly then, there was a gentle breeze in the air blowing the smog back to L.A., and Xan and I just had fun enjoying the scenery and one other, all that crap that I miss so much now. She was one of the first to be purged under the new regime. Gone by our last Christmas.

Xan and Xandry, polyandry.

Friday, November 26<u>th</u>

Reason to celebrate. I've now been treasoning for an entire month of Sundays. There's a freedom about this that I hadn't really anticipated. Somehow someone loses all sense of risk when one boldly goes where no one has gone before.

Ellison's gone fishin' for worms, I hear.

But Grace is back, Jack. Thank Fell. Spent Thanksgiving with her parents, she says. Her only relatives, she says. Her only relatives, I confirm.

I spy, Ty.

FYTTE THE FOURTH

Such, such were my dreams,
But now it all beseems
The phantom of a former life,
When administrative strife
Was the bread and butter
Of my day. When I could utter
A command and have it followed
Just like that, when grown men swallowed
Every insult and were glad, too glad
To serve me, good or bad:
Dead Fly, Dead Fly.

Monday, November 29th

Oh, terrible day. Oh, terrible way.
Can't write, Hite.

Tuesday, December 7th

A day that will live in infamy.
I could not write till now.
I'd just settled down to work last Monday when
the vestibule door slammed open, and two Saintpols

stomped in, guns drawn. I could see them from my office. They flanked the entryway while a sixsquad marched in, headed by the Sergeant-at-Arms. I glanced at the 'puter, but it was off, praise Fell. Without a word they seized Grace as she tried to back out of her chair. She screamed, just once, a brief cry of fright and despair.

I rushed forward to help.

"Wait," I said, "You can't...."

Wickhizer pierced me with his iron eyes *codé*.

"Do you object, Vicepro?"

Eternity froze.

"I, uh...," I stammered.

I looked desperately at Grace.

"Please," she mouthed.

Her face was white, her eyes wild, completely vulnerable. I would have given anything to take her right there, right then, in front of them all.

"Do you object?" the Sergeant repeated.

"No," I finally muttered, looking down at my soiled feet.

They dragged her out, beating her when she resisted.

"No," she moaned. "No no no no no."

What could I do, Stu? I gave her every expression of non-encouragement.

That afternoon I asked to see Provost right away, but he waited till 5:30, after his staff had gone home.

I didn't beat about the berry bush, either.

"What's going on?" I asked. "I'm...."

He waved me into silence, pointing pointedly to the

light, to his desk, and then to his ear in quick succession, and shaking his head.

"Sit, Vicepro. Sorry I am to inform you," he intoned, "that advocator Grace has been relocated for possible misguidance, having passed datanews to anti-Fellrads. We know someone is lib-leaking from this almighty and holy institution, and have gradually narrowed the source of that information to a modicum of rad-possibilities.

"Your predecessor was one such: his potentiality has now been much reduced. Your advocator is another. She will be sanctified by the appropriate authorities and either cleansed or corrected."

"But sir," I replied, "how can I do my job if I'm not kept informed...."

Provost leaned forward, glancing hither and yon with his cold gray eyes.

"I ken your situation, Vicepro," he said. "You will be brought into the Fellosophy in due course. However, you were given this holy office specifically because you could not have been the source of this info, having had no previous knowledge of or access to the material. That access must be restricted, at least until the source of the leak is found. If Miss Grace is albinized of these charges, she will be returned forthwith to your office. In the meantime, you may share my advocator."

He rose from his oversized chair.

"I'm having dinner with Chancel Gartendrech at seven," he said, "and he has asked me to include you in our little party. Meet me here at six-half."

I was stunned. I could only stammer my thanks.

Since I didn't own the clothes for such an occasion, nor the funds to buy them, I was consequently so nervous at the possibility of meeting Chancel socially that I scarcely could eat or speak throughout the entire evening. Every so often I'd realize that just picking at my elegantly-served plate might be construed as bad manners (or worse), and I'd quickly gobble down a few bites of whatever it was before drifting off again. I honestly have no idea what was served or what I said during that long night. I was in such a turmoil that it's a wonder I didn't piss my pants at some point.

I do remember one thing Chancel said, to some fat old broad sitting on my right. She had asked him how things were going at old Saints U., a typical outsider question, and he suddenly turned to her and grinned his thin grin.

"We're doing just fine," he said, "Except for the occasional malcontents, and when we're finished with them, they'll be doing just fine too."

She didn't say much the rest of the evening. She was dumb, but not *that* dumb.

I latterly detected a very ancient and fish-like smell emanating from her carcass.

* * * * * * *

I continued to slide through the week, papers just drifting into mounds all over my desk, and couldn't seem to concentrate on getting anything done. My interviews with supposed miscreants became no more

than *pro forma* sessions.

I no longer knew what was right or what was wrong, or what it was that I was supposed to be doing. I couldn't even use the 'puter, because the Saintpols were everywhere, coming and going, probing and prodding, often while I wasn't there. They obviously hadn't found their "leak," whoever it was, and for my own part, I hadn't yet figured out what was so goddam important about the University that the information would even be *worth* giving to the Underground.

Ah, yes, that dreaded "U" word, the one everyone tiptoes around. It was common knowledge, of course, even though no one talked about it directly. But I had never actually met anyone who'd had first-hand information about it.

Or had I? Who *were* these shades? What was their goal? What specifically had they done—or wanted to do? There were constant reports on the tube about various subversives being rounded up and shot or tortured or crucified (depending on the severity of their crimes), but never an exact rendition of what those supposed crimes had been, not in the detail *I* wanted, anyway. Awful things were awfully well hinted at all the time. It was enough that they were evil anti-Fellticans. Dr. Fell himself always spoke of them with compassion, exhorting us to reform these misguided folks who were hurting him (and us) so badly.

I keep wondering what's happened to Grace. Even though there was nothing I could have done to save her, I still feel somehow responsible for her.

I should have.... Could have.... Would have....
But I didn't, nosiree.

Wednesday, December 8th

The Vice Provost for Instructional Technology was taken today. A massive purge is underway. People are frightened of losing their jobs, their security, even their lives. Everyone watches everyone. All the time. I've ceased going to the Stu-U for lunch. The stress there has become almost unbearable, thick enough to slice, dice, and add to the menu, lightly-sautéed and -seasoned.

The leak leaketh still. I hear whispers, rumors of the Saintpols taking over the University, of some horrendous unnamed and unnamable scandal brewing, of...whatever.

No one really knows, do they? That's what makes it so much fun.

Ha ha ha.

I'm laughing now.

Later

Grace is back!! Thank Fell! Thank Great Fell!

Thursday, December 9th

Oh god, if there is a god, bless you for saving her! Grace looked terrible and wonderful all at the same time: worn, pale, ragged, very thin, with bandages covering

two of the fingers of her left hand. She wouldn't say what they'd done, or why. She only nodded when I asked her if she'd been cleared, if she was all right, and she wouldn't even look at me otherwise.

She just sits there staring at her desk. I don't really blame her. I don't. I know I betrayed her. Still, I'm glad she's alive. Maybe there's hope yet for this old, well-worn-out world.

Maybe.

FYTTE THE FIFTH

Ah, distinctly I remember,
It was in the dark September
That I came to old Cal State,
Young, oh so young, and never late,
Never late, no, never never late,
Until that day, wretched day,
When I read my cards, the tarot,
That said I should meet my fate
At old, too old, Cal State,
Three good years and ten,
They said, thirteen years, and then—
And then, welcome oblivion.

Friday, December 10th

Provost burst into my office at noon.

"They've arrested Tannenbaum," he gasped. His face was flushed and he was breathing heavily.

Tannenbaum was Captain of the campus branch of the Saintpols. So, even the cops weren't immune. This was beginning to get much more interesting.

"Wickhizer has been promoted Acting Captain," he added. "I think he may have arranged for his predeces-

sor's seizure. Madness reigns."

"What shall we do?" I inquired, all innocence and complicity.

He plopped down across from me, in the seat usually reserved for my inquisitees, rubbing one hand across his bald head, trying to move the few remaining wisps to cover an expanse they were never designed to fill. I had never seen him so obviously out of sync.

Then he pulled a small device out of his pocket, setting it on my desk. I could barely sense a high-pitched whining emanating from the instrument.

"That will protect us from hidden ears," Provost said.

There was a long pause, Klaus.

"We have no defense against rumor and innuendo," he continued. "The process may be careening past the ability of anyone to control it. Should something happen to me, you shall become the instrument of my revenge. If I am taken, go at once to my office. Tell the Saintpols that you must sequester the evidence there in order to present it before the Quisition. Order everyone out. Enter my 'puter. The password is the last fifteen letters of the third aphorism mounted on my wall, counting clockwise from the door. Reverse the letters, starting from the end.

"Copy the directory called 'Saints' onto a minidisk. Then type the word 'h-a-l-l-e-l-u-y-a-h,' that exact spelling and no other, and hit 'enter.' It will strip the entire drive clean. You can also set it to activate later.

"Keep the material stored only on the minidisk; do

not put it on your 'puter. Access the files by typing my name twice, the second time reversed, and do with the information what you will."

"But what about access to U-net?" I asked.

I had not yet been granted this privilege, customary to one of my standing.

He swallowed before replying. "User name: 'Rumpelstiltskin.' Password: 'Longyellowhair110248.'

"Since they can trace the ID of any machine accessing the Net, install this file first"—Bork handed me a disk—"It will change your ID number every few seconds, never giving the right one, confusing any simple effort to follow the connection back to you.

"But be thou warned: the central 'puter can overcome any such masquerade in roughly three minutes. Keep very careful track of the time, and never log on for more than sixty seconds at a stretch. Remember also to use this device"—he pointed to the silencer— "so the times you spend working on the 'puter cannot be coordinated with unauthorized entrance into the system."

"You seem very certain of your arrest," I stated, cheering internally at the possibilities.

"I believe that I know the name of the individual doing this," Provost said. "If I am right, he will move again soon, and have himself appointed to my position."

"If that should happen," I indicated, "I will take all appropriate steps."

Bork smiled for the first time in all my recollection

of him.

"I picked well when I chose you," he stated, "for I saw in you something of myself, and I was right once again."

I shuddered at the thought.

"Now, I have much to do if I am to avoid the fate that I have predicted for myself. I suggest that you come in tomorrow, just in case."

Later

My head was still throbbing from my conversation with Provost when Grace entered my office just before five.

"May I speak with you?" she asked.

"Of course," I responded, motioning her to take the seat by my desk.

The subtle scent of her slowly filled my nostrils, and I found myself excited by her closeness. I instinctively activated the dampening device that Bork had left me, and pulled my chair close to hers, directly facing her.

"How can I help you?" I inquired.

"Sir, I would like a leave of absence," she stated, "in order to visit my family."

"You saw your parents at Thanksgiving," I noted.

"Yes, but I...." She couldn't think of anything else to say.

"If I approved such a request without a compelling reason," I indicated, "I should be subject to scrutiny myself. Do you want that?"

"Why, no, sir," she said, surprised at this. "You've

been very kind to me, really, but I must, I have to get away from here."

"If anyone else heard these comments," I said, "you'd be subject to immediate re-arrest by the Saintpols."

"Not that, please!" she stated. "I just don't know what to do anymore."

Then she started to cry.

Well, what was an administrator to do? Someone had to comfort the poor girl.

So I took her in my arms and kissed away the tears, and after a minute or so she began kissing me back, and then I cleared some doodads off one corner of my desk, and she proved very convincingly that she wasn't quite the innocent girl she claimed to be.

Amazing Grace,
How sweet she is!

Saturday, December 11<u>th</u>

I normally stay away from CSU on weekends, but Provost had made clear my mandatory attendance today. So here I was, Buzz.

I started the day by installing the minidisk Bork had left me, and then I logged onto U-net. After checking the protocols, I immediately logged off again, and then went back into the system in normal mode.

"Rumpelstiltskin," indeed!

Suddenly a brand new vista revealed itself to me. Suddenly I understood something of what was happening here. Suddenly I began to see the greater

possibilities, particularly if I should ever gain access to Provost's secret files.

The personnel roster attracted my most immediate interest. Sixteen faculty and staff had been purged just in the last three months, from Parrott at the very bottom of the food chain to Vicepro Fernkorn, last week.

What did they have in common? I couldn't see a thing.

Many of the upper-level vacancies, except for Captain of the Saintpols, remained unfilled save by acting heads.

There was a subtle knock on my chamber door.

I quickly shut down the 'puter, put away the disks, buzzed the security panel to check visual, and was amazed to see Grace standing outside. I immediately let her in.

"What are you doing here today?" I asked.

"I knew you had to come, so I thought you might need my services," she replied. "In any case, I have nothing better to do with my time."

What a generous soul she was. What a giving, shining individual.

"Come over here," I said, smiling to myself, beckoning with my hands.

Oh yes, please do, Lou!

She ambled slowly over to my desk.

"No, here," I said, pointing to the near side.

She dutifully approached my large, leather-encrusted executive chair, my legacy of greatness, stopping right in front of me.

"Now close your eyes," I ordered.

When she complied, I let her stand there a moment, swaying slightly back and forth. She was about thirty years of age, with a light brown complexion completely swathed in a light brown dress that hung to her light brown ankles, covering her in the fashion prescribed by law.

Very, very carefully, as one would approach a shy animal, I leaned forward and touched her garment on both sides. Other than gasping out loud, she neither said anything to protest my action nor withdrew. Slowly, ever so slowly, I began bunching her skirt in my hands, pulling it upward inch by subtle inch, until the hem was hemmed well above her beautifully compact knees. Higher and higher it rose, but I was careful never actually to touch her skin.

When at last I could see what I was doing, when her light pink panties were finally revealed, I stopped. Her breath was coming more rapidly now, as she antici-pated my next move.

I grasped the sides of her underwear, and inched it down carefully over her broad ecru thighs. Once past the impediment, the garment slid all the way south. She even opened her legs a little to help. Both of us were huffing and puffing now. Blow the man down.

Then I touched her center, and she was coming in my hand, her body twitching uncontrollably with each successive *grand mal*.

Still, her eyes remained firmly closed.

See no evil, hear no evil, do no evil.

I let the folds of her dress flop loosely back over her pretty legs.

"You may go now," I said, the words faint but understandable.

She opened the orbs of her eyes, and bent down to retrieve her panties.

"Leave them," I ordered, and she complied.

What choice did she have?

I locked them carefully away in my desk.

> *Oh wicked wicked me,*
> *A rat ran up the tree.*
> *It found a hole to hide,*
> *It found a nut inside!*

Now I knew what I could do. Now I was ready. Oh yes, indeedy.

Goody goody gumdrops!

FYTTE THE SIXTH

And when at last I woke
God had laughed his cosmic joke,
And made me what I am today,
A fly, wretched fly, fey
Cousin to Archy and Mehitabel
Just a bug, a neer-do-well
Buzzing about the empty sky,
Seeking, looking, God knows why,
For some answer to my dreary fate,
Why, when I was never late,
I was damned to this faint
Existence.

Monday, December 13th

Now the shit really hitteth the fan, if you know what I mean. Nudge nudge, wink wink, and all that.

Provost was taken first thing this morning. Grace buzzed me at 9:15 with the news, and I rushed over right away to Bork's office, as I had promised. Herr Wickhizer, bless his rotten, ratty soul, was already rummaging through Provost's papers, looking for Fell knows what, his several goons keeping quarter time by

slapping their batons into their hairy palms.

"Captain Wickhizer," I intoned in my loudest of loud voices.

He stopped riffling through Bork's once-locked filing cabinet, and turned to face me.

"What the hell are you doing here?" he demanded.

"As Acting Provost"—I knew the regs ordained me such by virtue of my position, save only should Chancel contravene—"it will be my job to prosecute the accused. To do so effectively I must have first access to the evidence."

"What in blazes are you talking about?" Wickhizer snorted. "He's guilty as charged, and he'll be judged and sentenced tomorrow by the Faculty Senate. You know that. Your interference now could be considered complicity in his treason."

He nodded very slightly, and I felt my arms seized by two of his men. They were not gentle, Yentl.

I smiled toothily, which was not at all what he was expecting.

"You can remove the faculty without creating any ripples, Captain," I indicated, "but Provost is the second-ranking officer in this administration, and we cannot simply escort him stage left. We must observe procedures to ensure that his guilt is evident to everyone present. Where is thy warrant?"

I had the serious impression that I was the very first being ever to inquire for that most precious of precious documents. He reached into his back pocket and handed it over. I shook loose my arms to read it.

"Why, my dear Capitán," I said, in the most polite-but-firm tone that I could manage, "this document orders you to arrest Provost Bork. It says nothing about disturbing his office."

"What?" Wickhizer replied.

He grabbed the warrant out of my hands, almost tearing it in half. I honestly don't think he had ever actually read one during the entire course of his career.

"I'll be back," he finally stated, glaring at me with such hate that I had to activate my Teflon-coated, super-dooper, anti-fuzz energy shield just to survive the moment.

Bleep bleep bleep!

I continued smiling. I was becoming such a helpful person these days.

"I'll welcome your assistance," I noted.

He stormed out the door followed by his hairy Neanderthals.

I promptly secured the entrance, downloaded the necessary files from Bork's 'puter, set the worm to activate when the machine was turned on again, and then looked through the folders in that formerly impregnable filing cabinet. I was especially interested in some scurrilous material that I found on the Saintpols, which I duly salvaged for future use.

Before I left, I planted a few carefully prepared documents in Bork's file drawers. The entire operation took no more than five minutes.

Then I returned to my own office, and motioned Grace to join me in the inner sanctum.

I set the silencer, and asked her to sit down.

"Miss Smythe," I said, "you know that I saved you from the Saintpols."

She nodded, comprehension and gratitude making her suddenly blush with shame.

"How would you like some righteous vengeance for the unholy and unsanctified things they did to you?" I asked.

She nodded again.

"Do you know Sergeant Shibe?" I continued.

He was one of six or eight individuals with that rank on the campus force.

She nodded once more.

"What do you ken of his personal life?" I prodded.

"I, well sir, I believe...." She looked down at her lap. "I'm not sure what you want me to say, sir."

What a sweet thing she was, wholly unspoiled and wholly innocent, even after her unspeakable treatment by the pols. I really must promote her when all of this is finished.

"I want to know what his proclivities are," I indicated. "Do you understand what I mean?"

"I think so, sir," she replied. "Sergeant Shibe is a quiet man, neither mean nor abusive. I don't mean to imply that he's weak, but he's different from the rest of them."

"In what way?" I asked.

"Well, sir, he's, uh, he doesn't stare at my boobs all the time," she finally blurted out.

"Why do you think he reacts that way?" I pressed.

"I wouldn't know, sir," she stated. "He treats all the people equitably, I believe. Maybe he's just nice?"

"Let me see if I grok this correctly," I continued. "Are you saying he has no interest in women?"

"I, I...."

This was clearly a destination that she had never visited before.

"Grace?" I was relentless in my pursuit. "Please respond."

"Well, perhaps, sir."

"Stand up," I abruptly ordered.

"Yes, sir," she replied, rising from her seat.

"Remove your blouse," I told her.

She looked askance for a moment, blinked once or twice, and then carefully began undoing the buttons, one by one, first folding and then draping the garment over one edge of my desk.

Neat, Clete.

"Now your bra," I added.

She hesitated a moment, then dropped her gaze, and reached slowly around her back with both hands to unhook the catch. She slipped the straps off each shoulder, one at a time, and slid them down her lovely arms. I could already see the goose bumps forming. She let the brassiere drop forward, and added it to the pile on the desk.

She stood there for a moment, her breasts swinging free. She shivered in reaction.

"Let me have it," I stated, holding out my right hand. She picked up the bra, and I took the thing and

stashed it in my hidden cache. Then she covered her breasts with her arms, shaking all over.

"Stop that!" I ordered.

"Yes, sir," she replied, blushing as she dropped her hands to her sides.

It was the nipples that gave her away. They stood straight out, standing at attention.

"Tell me, Grace," I said. "Will you do anything that I ask you to do, whatever it might be, whenever I tell you to?" I asked.

"I, uh, y-yes, sir," she stammered.

"Why?" I inquired.

"Because you saved me," came the hurried reply, and then more slowly. "And because I must."

I waited another moment, watching how her quick breaths stirred those lovely, brown-topped mounds. She still wouldn't look at me.

"Raise your eyes," I ordered.

Then she stared straight into my soul, and something about those violet orbs mightily disturbed me.

"Very well," I finally said. "You may put your clothes back on now."

When she had finished, I ordered her to unfasten the top two buttons, allowing her blouse to reveal her cleavage to anyone with the slightest interest in it. Then I asked her to page Sergeant Shibe, but ordered her to remain in my office while I interviewed him.

Shibe was already on duty, as I was well aware, and so reported to me within fifteen minutes.

I motioned him to sit in front of my desk, and asked

Grace to pull a chair next to him to take notes. I made sure that he had a very clear view of the tops of her lovely appendages.

"Sergeant Shibe," I said, opening a file that I had confiscated from Provost's office, "I see here that you have served the University with distinction for some seven years."

"I have indeed, sir," he replied.

His cap was folded under his left arm, right where it should be. Military to the core, this one was.

"Sergeant, do you find Miss Smythe attractive?" I inquired.

"What?" he responded, looking at her very quickly, and then back at me again.

"I don't understand, sir."

"It's a simple question, really," I noted, smiling my toothy smile. "Do you find Miss Smythe attractive?"

"I guess so, sir," he indicated.

"Then reach over, unbutton her blouse, and fondle her breasts," I ordered.

He swallowed audibly.

"That, uh, that would be wrong, sir," he stated.

"Anything done on behalf of Dr. Fell and the California Saints University is *per se* righteous and proper, and that decision is mine, not yours, to make, Saintpol," I thundered. "Do it! *Do it now!*"

He put his funny little cap on the desk, and Grace simultaneously set aside her notepad. She stared impassively at me while he began undoing her garment. His fingers were trembling so hard he could barely control

them. Finally, the rest of the buttons were loosed.

"Shibe!" I demanded again.

He reached inside her open blouse and touched her left breast. He rubbed it perfunctorily a few times before quickly withdrawing his hand, shaking it as if it had been singed.

"Sergeant," I said, "you do not seem to be enjoying your work."

"No sir," he replied.

"According to my information," I continued, looking down at the file spread in front of me, "based on data compiled by Herr Wickhizer—which makes it true, doesn't it?—you have *never* preferred the company of women."

Shibe suddenly looked as if he had swallowed a toad, Joad.

"That's a damned lie, sir!" he finally ejaculated, after a twenty-second pause.

"You waited a bit too long there, Sergeant," I indicated. "Sorry, but I will regard that as a confirmation. Never fear, my dear Shibe, this will become our little secret, just between the three of us. Unlike several of my more hidebound colleagues, I believe that God created each and every one of us in his own image, even those who, shall we say, have strayed slightly from the path of righteousness."

He slumped down completely in his chair, his face gone white.

"That's, uh, that's very big of you, sir," he stated.

"Not especially," I replied. "I've decided to make the

world safe for you, Sergeant, not from you, but I really do need your help to accomplish it. I'm sure you'll agree that this is a task well worth doing."

His face suddenly lit up as he realized that I was dead serious.

Dead, Fred, dead.

There's nothing like the prospect of a little freedom to set a condemned man's heart a-dancin'.

"I have uncovered evidence that Captain Wickhizer has been leaking information to the underground."

I pointed to the stack of papers piled in front of me.

"No!" both of them chimed in.

"Yes," I said, "and I was as amazed as you at the Captain's complicity. But who else would have had access on a continual basis to the very core of our data systems? Captain Wickhizer has directly profited by the discreditation of his superior, and now he stands to rise again by his denunciation of Provost."

"But if what you say is true," Shibe replied, "then we must take steps immediately to save Dr. Bork."

"Alas," I stated, "that such were possible. Unfortunately, we must proceed very cautiously, or we ourselves will be arrested and denounced. My question to you is this, Shibe: can you put together a squad of Saintpols who are irrefutably and undeniably loyal only to you?"

Shibe ran his hand back over his close-cropped hair, and thought for a moment.

"I believe I can count on perhaps a dozen men that would be true to me under any circumstance," he indi-

cated. "No more than that, at least initially."

"That's quite sufficient," I stated. "I will let you know the particulars in due course. In the meantime, Sergeant, I might mention that should I suddenly disappear or be arrested, the facts regarding your case shall be automatically and widely disseminated. Do you understand?"

He looked down at the floor.

"I do," he said.

"Then we have a bargain," I replied, holding out my hand. He took it reluctantly, then tried to leave.

"Sergeant," I stated.

He looked up at me.

"I don't insist that you like me. But you must remember at all times that your career will rise or fall with mine, and that betrayal must mean a remarkably unpleasant death for both you and your family. Unwholesome moral tendencies are an automatic writ to expunge an entire bloodline. But then, you already know that, don't you?"

I smiled once more.

"Dis-*missed*!" I ordered.

He came promptly to attention, pivoted perfectly, and then exited the room, slamming the door tightly behind him.

Grace gazed upon me with new wonder, her mouth and blouse both gaping wide. Then she rose and slowly sloughed off her upper garment, and eased her skirt down over her wide hips; she stood there with her legs slightly akimbo, utterly beautiful, utterly open unto

me.

"Love me," she implored.

Whatever was a Fella to do?

I took my courage in both hands, and piled the faggots on the fire.

I kissed her once and then kissed her hard twice,
I kissed her again, which added some spice,
I kissed her once more, she kissed me right back,
She kissed me so hard, I fell down her crack!
I kissed her button, and then I sure knew,
That kissing a girl will bring on the dew,
I kissed her all over, opened her wide,
And into her tunnel I let Johnny slide,
I pushed and I pulled, she swallowed me up,
I gave all I had, and filled up the cup,
And then she did smile, and said, "That's just ten,
Come on now, sweetie, let's do it again!"

Tuesday, December 14th

The Faculty Senate met every week on Tuesdays, just after lunch, and on this particular Tuesday afternoon I was prepared, my friends, oh yes I was.

Earlier in the day I had directed Sergeant Shibe to sequester the contents of Provost's locked filing cabinet, and to bring the carefully sealed and marked boxes directly to me. He had, of course, complied. Then I gave him a new set of orders, which he assured me he would follow exactly as outlined.

I spent an hour in the morning sitting at the 'puter,

transferring data from Provost's encrypted files to selected recipients. Where necessary, I altered specifics to correspond with the new needs of the University.

If Fellosophy tells us aught of truth, it's this: the ends *do* justify the means. Always.

I was ready.

The Senate consisted of thirty representatives: ten faculty, two each from the five colleges; ten administrators, two each from the five divisions; five staff members; and five key administrative officers. My position as Acting Provost entitled me to an A.O.'s seat, but I had previously served as a faculty rep for three or four years, so I knew the drill very well.

"In the name of Fell," the Chairman squeaked, and we all bowed our heads while he droned on and on about the Greater Fellian Revolution and the glorious benefits we had all reaped therefrom.

A few of us, anyway.

After each of the division heads, plus myself and Chancel, had made brief presentations concerning the progress made since our last confab, held just a week ago (time really *does* fly when you're having fun), we were ready for new business.

Captain Wickhizer sat at the round table as an active participant, although he still held the position of Senate Sergeant-at-Arms. He was just about to raise the issue of Provost's trial and condemnation when I elevated my right hand.

"Actingpro?" said the Chairman.

"I want to commend Nickson Wickhizer for his

diligence in pursuing the enemies of Fell," I intoned. "He has earned our kudos and heartfelt thanks for his earnest efforts on His behalf. Therefore, I move that we suspend the rules and confirm him in his rank of Captain of the Cal Saintpols."

"Without dissent, it is so ordered," proclaimed Chairman Churchyard, looking around the table for nonexistent commentary.

"Let it be recorded," he ordered the Secretary.

Then he banged his gavel down most mightily, again and again, trying to wake the dead.

"Is there any new business?" he inquired.

Wickhizer raised his hand.

"Yes, Captain," Churchyard acknowledged.

"I hereby charge Provost Bork with treason against the University and with anti-Fellosophical thought," he blurted out, all in one breath.

"Point of order," I interjected.

"Yes, Actingpro?" the Chair stated.

"Senate Rule 1359.21572 clearly states that no one may serve simultaneously as a Senator and as a Senate employee," I said. "Therefore, Captain Wickhizer is automatically excluded from the position of Sergeant-at-Arms of this august body."

I nodded with respect in his direction.

"Further," I continued, "this position may only be filled by an accredited officer of the Saintpols. I therefore nominate Hamilcar Shibe to be the new Sergeant-at-Arms of the Faculty Senate."

Everyone began talking at once, which meant, of

course, that no one could really be heard. I just sat there and smirked. Wickhizer was only now beginning to realize how neatly I had forked his position.

"Wait a minute." The good Captain finally made himself heard.

"Just wait a minute!" he repeated, banging his right fist on the table until he got everyone's attention. "No one has consulted me about this proposal. This is my area of responsibility. I move that the nomination be tabled until next week."

"I certainly can have no objection to Captain Wickhizer's request," I responded, "even though I believe that Sergeant Shibe has earned the respect of the entire campus community"—I noticed several heads around the table bobbing up and down in agreement—"and deserves the opportunity to expand upon his already proven abilities. However, I should be utterly derelict in my own responsibilities if I failed to point out to this ancient fraternity that the postponement of what must certainly be a *pro forma* confirmation of a dedicated police officer's new assignment has certain other political repercussions.

"For example, Herr Wickhizer lacks the authority to charge Provost with anything. Only the Senate Sergeant-at-Arms can do that"—the murmuring around the table suddenly grew an octave—"and I believe that we must consider the effect on the University if the trial and condemnation of Provost Bork is unduly delayed. I therefore move suspension of the rules, and a confirmation of Sergeant Shibe as Acting Sergeant-

at-Arms of the Faculty Senate, until the position can be permanently filled."

I sat back in my chair, thoroughly satisfied with the way the proceedings were unraveling. Wickhizer looked utterly out of his depth. I had to keep him continually off guard.

"Captain Wickhizer?" the Chairman intoned, seeking the Saintpol's response.

"I th-think...," he stuttered, then cleared his throat, trying to consider carefully before he spoke.

"Very well," he continued, "I will not object, so long as it is understood by the Senate that this is a temporary appointment, made in the interest of bringing those actions pending before this body to their swift and ultimate conclusion."

"Any other comments?" Churchyard inquired. "Hearing none," he stated, banging his gavel, "it is so ordered. Sergeant Shibe, you may approach the dais."

Shibe marched in, looking like the martinet he was, but making an excellent impression on the hidebound members of the High Holy Senate.

"Sir!" he barked.

"If you please, Captain," the Chair motioned, and Wickhizer passed his staff of office down the table.

"It is my privilege to confer upon you this great honor, Sergeant. Act wisely and to the benefit of Dr. Fell and California Saints University."

"I hear and obey, Chairman," the new Sergeant-at-Arms stated, saluting in turn both the Senate Chair, the Captain of the Saintpols, and Chancel.

"Now I do charge Provost Bork with treason against the University and with anti-Fellosophical thought."

"Is there any objection?" Churchyard asked. "Hearing none, the charges are ordered recorded by the Secretary. Sergeant-at-Arms, escort the prisoner to the bar."

Shibe promptly exited the room, and returned a few minutes later, leading a sixsquad surrounding and encompassing the former Provost.

Bork had been diminished in just a day to a caricature of himself. His formerly immaculate suit was now tattered and soiled, and one eye was so swollen from repeated beatings that he could scarcely open it. He limped over to the cage.

I rose to my feet, and straightened my collar before proceeding.

"Harminius Bork," I droned, "you have been charged with crimes against Fell. How dost thou plead?"

"Guilty," he said.

There were gasps of astonishment all around the table. Even Wickhizer seemed nonplussed.

"You understand fully the consequences of your plea?" I stated.

"I do."

"Before I pass sentence," I intoned, "is there anything you wish to say?"

"I plead extenuating circumstances, in that I was led from the straight and narrow way through the corruption of several of my colleagues."

"Who *are* these individuals?" I inquired.

We knew our roles very well indeed.

"The Vicepro for Security and Sanctification"—another series of inhalations and exhalations, plus a loudly brayed *"No!"*—"and the Chief of the Saintpols, Captain Wickhizer."

"What!" came the latter's roar. "This is outrageous!"

"Pending investigation," I said, "I hereby order the arrest without bail of Dell O'Dell and Nickson Wickhizer. The exercise of their offices is immediately suspended until their trials, set for a week hence."

The uproar was general now, but no one could do a thing about my little *coup* without themselves being accused, and everyone knew it. Chancel, having said nothing throughout the development of our drama in *realpolitik*, just smiled his appreciation at what I had done.

Smile all you want, cocksucker, I thought to myself. *You won't be smiling long.*

While everyone was trying to take stock, Shibe marched in another six of his men, and had his two squads surround and disarm the prisoners before they had time to react. He caught my eye, and I nodded slightly in return. He knew what to do. Then I looked back at Provost, and raised one eyebrow. He also nodded.

When I had restored order, and Shibe had returned with his double squad of loyal Saintpols, I banged on the table to garner everyone's attention.

"We have a trial to complete," I indicated, and motioned everyone to sit down.

When they were seated again, I proceeded.

"Harminius Bork, former Provost of California Saints University," I stated, "in recognition of the many services you have contributed to this institution, I hereby sentence you to death by firing squad, execution to be accomplished as soon as you have provided evidence in the case of the University vs. O'Dell and Wickhizer. May Fell have mercy on your soul!"

"Amen," the Senate intoned.

"Take the prisoner away," I ordered Sergeant Shibe.

As soon as he had left the room, I once again asked for the floor.

"I hereby nominate Sergeant Shibe to be Acting Captain of the Saintpols."

Whatever could have been more appropriate, my dearies?

The Chairman again looked over the august collection of mealy-mouthed halfwits scattered before him.

"Hearing no objection," he stated, "it is so ordered."

"I further move that the duties of the Vice Provost for Security and Sanctification be temporarily placed under the aegis of the office of Provost of the University," I said.

"Hearing no objection...."

"I further move that the Office of Provost of the University be confirmed upon the present occupant of that chair," I said.

"Hearing no objection...."

"I further move that...."

All in all, it was a very good day.

O'Dell and Wickhizer, on the other hand, did not have a good day. In fact, they had no more days left at all.

The world is not thy friend, Oh Wickhizer, nor even the world's law.

FYTTE THE SEVENTH

This bluebottle paint
Now clothes this wretched crate,
And I spend my days butting my pate
Against screen doors and glass panes,
Numbing, dumbing what few brains
I have left, looking for Dr. K.
And Mr. B., to have one final say,
One last bite, if I may,
At the administrative neck,
And all the garbage, all the dreck,
That I cheerfully ate along the way.
Which is why, I cry,
God made me fly,
Dead Fly.

Wednesday, December 15th

The next morning, I found a bouquet of flowers standing on the center of my desk, placed there by my lovely and thoughtful advocator. There were fresh lilies and carnations and some other growths that I failed to recognize. I kissed Grace a good one on her lips when

I saw her, smudging her paint, and she responded with even more energy of her own. Blessèd be!

Then we set about moving into my new suite of offices, those which had formerly belonged to Provost Bork. I made certain that Dr. B.'s personal effects were carefully gathered together and dispatched to his incipient widow. The other details I left to Grace.

At the bottom of the second drawer on the right in Bork's desk, I found a small, yellowed piece of paper taped to the back edge. I carefully retrieved it. It sounded vaguely familiar:

Great fleas have little fleas upon their backs to bite
  'em,
And little fleas have lesser fleas, and so ad infinitum.

What did it mean? Why was it there?

I took that question with me that very afternoon on my final visit to Harminius Bork, late Provost of California Saints University, now temporarily resident in a cell in the Schicklgruber Building on the opposite side of campus.

I walked the quarter mile alone, neither desiring any company nor seeking idle conversation. I was thinking about what yet needed to be done to transform our modest University into a modern, growing educational establishment of the first rank. The initial step was obvious, but what came afterwards?

The Schicklgruber Building was round, squat, and windowless, clothed in the gray concrete of state structures, and utterly without a charm of any kind. A

single large chimney poked its ugly head up through the center of the complex, sticking some thirty feet above the roof. The height was necessary to keep the smell away from campus.

I first sought out my old friend Wickhizer.

"What do *you* want?" he growled.

He was shackled to one wall of his cell, unable to move his arms enough even to scratch his nose.

"I just thought I'd share some information with you before you pass into that darkest of dark nights," I said.

"Why bother?" he retorted.

"Because," I responded, "because I only did to you what you would have done to me, within a day or two. If you're looking for a rescue, my friend, you should understand that your cohorts have either been reassigned or redistributed, piece by piece, and thus are no longer in a position to aid your potential comeback. This really is your final final appearance on the political stage. You're about to exit, stage left."

"So?"

He seemed unconcerned by his defeat.

"So, there'll be no trial," I noted, "as you might already have guessed. You and O'Dell will try to escape sometime during the night, one of these nights, and, regretably, you'll fail once again.

"But there *is* something positive that you can yet contribute to this world, if you so choose."

"Why should I?" he said.

"Several reasons, actually," I responded.

I was thoroughly enjoying myself.

"First, I'm willing to recommend that your wife be given a pension based on your twenty-two years of service to Fell and State"—I pulled a paper from my vest, and pressed it flat against the scanner, so that the contents would flash on the large screen mounted on one wall of the cell—"As you can see, it is a generous, lifetime offer, already signed, sealed, and certified. I can have it notarized and filed on this very console, right before your eyes, and you can die with the assurance that you've provided something fine for your next of kin.

"If, on the other hand, you should choose not to cooperate, I can also make certain that your son will thoroughly enjoy a decade of servitude down in Yucatán, and that your two daughters will be drafted into the Social Services Corps, providing intimate solace to our love-sick soldiers languishing overseas.

"But there's another reason, too. I would think you would want one more chance to screw the individual who actually put you in this situation."

"What are you talking about? It was *you*."

His voice revealed a certain level of uncertainty to the subtle ear.

"Was it?" I countered. "Thinkest thou for a moment, dead old Wick. Did I, do I, could I, have had the power and ability to accomplish this kind of sweep in just a few weeks time? Well, I rather think not, and neither do you in your own heart of hearts. Any damn fool can see that a mere faculty member—and remember, that's all I was until just a month ago—could never

have proceeded on this scale without the backing of a high-ranking member of the administration. You already know who's been purged. Now tell me something, Wickhizer: who's left?"

"I'll be damned," he muttered to himself, shaking his head.

"What do you want me to do?" he finally stated.

"Just give me a little information," I responded, "and a notarized statement of accusation. That's all I ask. Now, that's not so much, is it? Shall I file this document on your behalf?"

I waved the pension in front of the iron bars.

"File it!" he barked. "I'll do anything you want."

"Excellent," I replied. "It's really good to see that even you have a streak of altruism buried deep beneath that ugly exterior."

I shall not repeat his profanity-laced response.

An hour later, after I'd finished business with Wickhizer, I paid my last respects to my mentor, Provost Bork. He was in surprisingly good spirits, considering. I mentioned the little poem to him.

"Oh, you found that, did you?" he chuckled. "Well, it's rather good advice. Always watch your back. Remember, you can eliminate everyone in the world but your ultimate successor. Someone will eventually take your place, and you can't prevent that. In fact, you can do no more than slant the outcome a bit.

"You still have a wee bit of a problem, of course," he continued. "*I'm* not the traitor, and I'm reasonably certain that Wickhizer isn't, either. So who's been

leaking material to the Underground?"

"What material?" I asked. "I've been trying to think what information could have made any difference to the future of the University, and I admit to being completely at a loss."

"It was small things at first," Bork indicated, "starting about a year ago. Private messages sent from one Vicepro to another began being publicly posted to the campus net. The common recipient was finally purged, and the leak stopped for several months. Then a faculty member who was on the verge of being radicated was informed of that fact in advance, by receiving a copy of a *very* confidential memorandum, and he was able to kill several members of the administration before he was shot down by the Saintpols. You will recall the incident, I'm sure."

I did indeed. It had happened just after school started in September. They said the man had gone totally starko. Afterwards, campus security had been considerably tightened.

"Postings would stop for a time, and then start up again at random," he continued. "We could never find a pattern to it. All we knew for certain was that it had to be one of us. We were able to confirm this during one of the routine external power outages, in the course of which another leak occurred. All of the postings originated from within the U-net, not outside the University. Things began to deteriorate seriously about a month ago, and you know the rest."

"Well," I muttered, "if it wasn't you, and it wasn't

me, then who was it?"

"That, as they say," the former Provost stated, "is the million-dollar question. That's why I tell you to continue exercising supreme caution. You've done very well in just a short period of time. Do not let your success go to your head. Some of it is always luck. Remember that.

"Now," he added, "are you happy with what I've given you?"

"Indeed," I replied.

"Then I presume my usefulness to you has now been exceeded by the threat I pose," he said.

I just nodded my head in commiseration.

"No matter," he indicated. "I had a good run. You will need to be very lucky indeed to remain on top for as long. I will not ask you what you intend to do. That part is obvious. *Ave utque vale*, my friend."

"And to you," I responded.

Then I left, never looking back. Harminius Bork would be "vanished" before morning.

Back at my office, I sat down in front of my 'puter, and powered up the console. Two words in red, 108-point type began flashing on my screen:

DEAD
FLY

I buzzed Grace, and asked her to page Captain Shibe. When he reported, I bade them both enter my new office, and showed them my terminal.

"What does it mean?" Shibe inquired.

"Never mind that," I stated. "I didn't put it there. Who did?"

They both looked at each other, and I knew what they were thinking. I pressed the button underneath my desk that swung the door shut and locked it.

"Shibe," I said, "someone has broken into my terminal, probably from outside. There has been a security breach," I repeated. "I want to know who, how, when, what, and why."

"Yes, sir," he responded, completely without enthusiasm.

I opened a drawer, and set a long, black, thick thermometer on the desk. Shibe stared at it in puzzlement.

My advocator was standing closest to me on the left, with the Saintpol just beyond her.

"Grace," I ordered, "bend over my desk."

She obeyed me without question, bless her sooty soul.

I suddenly flung her skirt up over her back, revealing a completely bare bottom—no underwear.

"Shibe, take Miss Smythe's temperature," I commanded.

"What do you mean, sir?" His voice trembled almost as much as his hand.

"You heard me," I said. "Stick it up her ass."

"That would be, uh...."

He suddenly realized what he was saying, and turned completely pale.

"Sir, I...."

"Just do it, *Acting* Captain," I stated.

"Very well, sir."

His shoulders slumped as he very gently picked up the device, and began working it slowly into her, twirling it every time he met resistance. Grace began panting again. Her eyes closed completely. Finally, he had all but the end inserted.

"Now hold it there," I ordered, "and rub her underneath."

Without comment, he obeyed me, and continued until she started to come. Then I ordered him to stop, and he watched as the thermometer gradually was squeezed out.

"What's the temperature?" I inquired.

"99°," he responded, after he had gingerly removed the thing.

"Things are heating up all over," I noted, patting Grace's delicate ass and pulling her skirt back down to cover her from prying eyes.

"Now find me that leak," I ordered.

"Yes, sir," he said, and ran from the room.

As soon as he had gone, Grace turned around, raised her skirt again, and said, "Temperature's rising, sir."

Then she spread her legs, and daintily began to play with herself.

Well, someone had to cool her off. It was just the gentlemanly thing to do.

Thursday, December 16th

First thing this morning I received an invitation for a private dinner with Chancel Gartendrech on Friday

evening. I could bring one guest. I immediately invited Lady Grace, who was pleased to accept.

"Do you have something appropriate to wear?" I inquired.

"How do you mean, sir?" she asked, in between licks.

I was finding it rather difficult to concentrate at about this time, since things were starting to come to a head. My seven years of enforced abstinence were now being followed by seven years of abundance.

Grace was doing her communicating in quite another way, and doing it well too—the girl had skills that I never had found posted in her résumé—and I was just about to compliment her in the most intimate way possible when suddenly there flashed on the 'puter screen three more scarlet words:

DEAD
FUCKING
FLY

"Shit!" I yelled, and Grace almost did me permanent damage.

"Shit!" I yelled again, and her head bobbed up as I deflated.

"What's the matter?" she asked, all concern now.

"Look!" I said, pointing with my thing at the screen. "Look!"

"Oh," she replied, turning her head. "Oh."

Then she looked down at me again, saw that there was no point at all in proceeding, and got up.

"Sorry," she said. "Sorry."

I zipped up my trousers, and again called security, but they found nothing, as usual.

A little later in the day, Grace handed me a printout of the daily campus rag.

"O'DELL AND WICKHIZER SHOT WHILE ESCAPING!"

the headline shouted.

"BORK EXECUTED FOR ANTI-FELLTICANISM."

That made me feel a little better, to be sure, and I asked for my morning cup of *chai*. The rest of the day passed uneventfully. A purge here, an execution there, hey, it was all grist for the mill.

> *Up and down the street I run,*
> *All I have is fun fun fun,*
> *Torching this and killing that,*
> *Fucking puss and squishing cat,*
> *Smashing kids and eating dog,*
> *Banging wives and drinking nog,*
> *I spit, piss, and shoot my gun,*
> *All I have is fun fun fun.*

Friday, December 17th

I spent the morning preparing for the evening. This included some surfing, some reading, being measured

for a suit, getting into my secret cache, and a few other things.

A good little boy scout am I, I cry.

After lunch Grace modelled the formal dress she proposed to wear to our *soirée* this evening. I was somewhat disappointed, however, to find that it fell directly to her ankles, and completely covered her cleavage, although her unfettered breasts could still be detected by the discerning eye, moving fetchingly and independently beneath the light fabric. I think she saw right through me, though, because she smiled and asked if I'd like a drink of water.

Nothing could have been further from my wants or desires at that place and time, and I immediately said so.

She just smiled again, went into the small bathroom alcove off my office, and brought back a brimming glass.

"Come here," she ordered.

I complied, standing in front of her.

She dipped two fingers of my right hand into the cup, and then placed them over her left breast, asking me to touch the nipple.

I was utterly astonished at the result. The moistened fabric suddenly became transparent where I was rubbing, and I could clearly see the small brown aureole and its little soldier standing at attention. I saluted it in the best way I knew how.

Then I tried the other side. Same result. Gee, a boy could learn something here.

She put the glass down on the floor, did something magical to the top of the dress, and the whole thing slid off her in one motion. It was breathtaking. I felt like Livingstone exploring the upper reaches of the Nile.

"Well just don't stand there," she said. "We must all give our best for Dr. Fell."

It's a hard life, but someone has to do it.

Later

A limousine called for us at seven. There was a partially opaque plastic barrier between the passengers and driver, and Grace teased the poor man by pulling up her dress and flashing him. I was greatly amused. There was nothing he could say or do, of course. He was just another dumb laborer, a Felloslave justly serving out his interminable time for some unknown and unknowable petty offense.

Chancel's home had been erected on Coyote Hill on the back side of campus. A little piece of rustic wilderness had been mercilessly planed right off, and a monstrosity of a mansion plopped on the slopes in its place, slopping up and down here and there as Fell had seen fit. A paved drive brought us to the base of the hill, where a small elevator lifted us 200 feet to the main entrance. Grace made certain that I had a great view of the view.

Chancel welcomed us personally, making apologies for the absence of Madame G., who was visiting their daughter in Cleveland for the upcoming New Year holiday. It would just be us three for dinner, he noted,

and hoped we wouldn't be disappointed.

No, indeedy.

The ambiance of the place was overwhelming, obviously intended to make an impression on the uninitiated. Everywhere the walls and *décor* screamed money and power, power and money, and all the goodies that provide accessories to the grotesquely rich. I saw classic artwork that I knew must have been taken from the oldest museums of Europe, with scarcely a by-your-leave to the original owners. Gartendrech had been Chancel for eight years now, and clearly had profited from the experience.

"You like?" he said, pointing to an oversized nude by one of the great masters.

"Yes," Grace replied, her mouth slightly open, her precise tongue licking her ruby lips.

The servants were quietly competent, fading into the background when not needed.

The meal was rich beyond belief to one used to shortages and constant excuses at the local markets. Fresh fruit imported from South America, fresh beef from Australia, fresh vegetables from the best surviving fields of Europe, everything that one could want was made available to us, in generous proportions and beautiful servings. I was beginning to feel like the Crown Prince of some near eastern monarchy.

After dessert, Chancel dismissed the servants for the night, indicating that they could finish cleaning up in the morning, and then got down to business.

"I have been impressed with the way you've handled

yourself these past weeks, Provost," he stated, pouring out a glass of port for himself and me, and ice water for the lady when she declined the spirits.

"You have moved quickly and firmly to meet the threat against our august institution, and I am confident that your actions will prove successful. Have there been any further attacks on our network?"

"Absolutely not," I lied. I was getting very good at this.

"I am assiduously working with Acting Captain Shibe, Miss Smythe here, and several of our technicians to ensure that the U-net remains safe. But you must understand, Chancel, that ours is an evolving technology, and that renewed attacks can come at any time. We must maintain our vigilance."

My bullshitometer was bursting right through the top of the old glass now. How this old fart could buy any of this crap was quite beyond me. But buy it he did!

"Excellent," Gartendrech responded. "Thoroughly excellent. And what are your thoughts on the subject, Miss Smythe?" he inquired.

"I follow the lead of my Provost in everything," she demurred, smiling slightly as she sipped her water.

I noticed him watching the wobble of her pointy breasts under the gown, and nodded at her slightly.

Suddenly she managed to spill the entire contents of her glass right down the front of her, and began pawing at her dress, effectively spreading the wetness wherever she wanted it to go.

"Oh, oh, oh!" she cried. "Oh, help me, Chancel."

I could see her boobs swinging back and forth as she daubed at them, the nipples clearly visible now as they pressed strikingly against the translucent fabric. They were certainly a mystical revelation to Gartendrech. I thought the old fart was going to have a heart attack.

"My, my, my," he exclaimed. "Oh my, please, please let me assist you, Miss Smythe."

He was soon brushing at the dainty gown with his napkin, while Grace was leaking tears from both eyes. What a classic performance! I felt like clapping, but instead muttered something about finding the rest-room, and headed off on my own expedition into the wilderness, leaving the two of them to work things out.

First stop was the main bedroom. Earlier that day I had retrieved my advocator's slightly used underwear from my secret cache, and now I tossed Grace's crumpled bra and panties under Chancel's bed. I tried to get them right beneath the center, where they would less likely be seen by the staff or scooped up in a routine cleaning.

Then I looked for the office-away-from-office that I knew Chancel had located nearby, and found it right next door. The entrance was locked, of course, but I had already anticipated this, and had come prepared with a little help from Captain Shibe. I now powered up Gartendrech's personal 'puter, and directly down-loaded a couple of things that I didn't want to risk trans-mitting over U-net. Finally, I accessed the Chancel's locked file cabinet, and inserted a few specially-

prepared sheets deep within the bowels of one very large folder, where they probably wouldn't be noticed for quite some time—unless someone knew precisely what they were looking for.

I made certain that everything was put back exactly the way it had been, and then I headed for the dining room again. No more than ten or fifteen minutes had elapsed, and I was reasonably certain that no one had espied my brief machinations.

By this time my dear little resourceful darling was perched quite nude on Chancel's lap, thanking him for his assistance in the only way she knew how, her arms around his scrawny neck, and he was diddling her with great finesse for such an old geezer, his shirt and pants already disheveled and open wide. I lingered in the shadows of the adjoining room, and used a pocket digital camera to take several classic shots that clearly revealed his straining face and her lush, responsive body, without, however, directly displaying her own visage. Still, it would be quite obvious even to the dumbest of the dumb that this was *not* the elderly Mrs. Gartendrech. I used up the battery for an entire series of photographs before pocketing the device and re-entering the room.

He tried to get up when he saw me, but only managed to look excessively silly.

"I, umm...," he sputtered.

"Please, feel free," I countered. I could afford to be generous. "Those in the service of Fell and the State get little enough reward for their efforts. I find it quite

commendable that you would take the time personally to instruct this young lady, particularly when you have such onerous duties to uphold."

"Very true," he admitted, and then gasped when she jumped off his lap, and bent her head down upon him.

Still Later

On the short limo trip back to the campus, Grace looked like the cat that had bagged the canary.

"Did you get what you wanted?" she inquired.

She was putting her luscious hair back in order while she talked.

"Yes, indeedy," I replied, "I think Dr. Gartendrech will soon have some new fields to tend. How about you?"

"I learned a great deal," she murmured. "He thinks to purge you as soon as he can, possibly at the next Senate meeting. He sees you as a threat to his continued rule here. Of course, he didn't state that explicitly. He promises to make me his mistress, if only...."

"Oh, joy!" I said, and we both laughed.

"And what will *you* make me?" she inquired.

"Sore," I said, reaching under her dress.

"Oh, my," Grace stated, "Whatever are you doing, my Provost?"

"Just what comes naturally," I noted.

> *Randy Andy, cotton candy,*
> *Chocolate's sweet, girls are dandy.*

FYTTE THE EIGHTH

I saw this gleaming place,
This shining, lovely space,
Filled with gold and light,
And toward it I took flight,
And realized all too late,
This really was my fate:
To plunge into the shimmering deep,
And naught but silences to keep.

Saturday, December 18<u>th</u>

Another Saturday session. Gad, Chad, I'm such a dedicated employee.

I insisted, of course, that Shibe and Grace both be present. Our little coterie of conspirators. This much and no more. I had half a notion to force the good Captain to fuck the luscious Miss G. right there in my presence, but after some due consideration, I thought that putting him into such an unnatural position might well send him right over the proverbial edge. I wanted to keep him resentful and bitter, all right, but also firmly leashed. It was a dangerous game that I was playing. I needed him right now, and he was just vulnerable

enough to play along, if I handled him right.

So I spent the morning reviewing the situation with them. I had incontrovertible evidence, I said, that Chancel was the traitor we had all been seeking.

"No," came the low groans of protestation, particularly from Shibe.

"Indeed," I said, "and it is our responsibility, and no one else's, to do something about it. Further," I continued, "Grace has discovered that Chancel intends to move against us on Tuesday at the Senate meeting. I don't have to tell you what that means."

I didn't, either. They both knew that if I fell, death and torture awaited anyone who had actively assisted me. I also made sure that Shibe was aware that certain defamatory documents concerning him would be automatically leaked unless I continued in office. Perpetually.

"So, what to do is the question on the table," I stated. "Captain Shibe, it's obvious to me that Chancel cannot proceed without an accuser in place. He must either try to subvert you or do what we did: supplant you with another. What are his options?"

"Well, sir," Shibe pondered, "as you know, I have been gradually replacing Wickhizer's supporters with my own, but it's a slow and tedious process. The obvious trouble-makers are gone, but there remain four old-line Sergeants with their own loyal squadrons. We must name one of them Sergeant-at-Arms on Tuesday. That position will greatly increase the power of the new occupant."

"Then that's the key," I indicated. "We must absolutely subvert the process. Do you have someone in your own squad who would be 100% loyal, and who has the experience to be advanced to SAT?"

"Tostig," he replied. "He's a five-year man, and one of my, uh, compatriots."

"You mean he's queer," I replied.

"Yes, sir."

"Can you control him?" I continued. "Can you make him understand what's at stake here?"

"I can, sir, but you must promise me something in return," Shibe said.

"The worm turneth, eh, Captain?" I stated, looking him straight in the eye. He looked right back. "So you have some gumption after all, Shibe. Very well, what do you want?"

"An end to the public persecutions, at least in those areas under your command," he responded. "That's all I ask. Nothing for me personally."

I propped my chin in my hands and thought about the situation for a moment. I could still make him screw Grace, but it probably wouldn't help matters any. I'd gone about as far as I could go with him and still keep him loyal. I didn't especially like starting down this particular path, but I didn't see that I had much choice.

"All right, Shibe, you've got a deal," I promised. "No persecutions as long as I'm in charge. And you've got a witness."

I nodded my head in Grace's direction.

"Now, there's something else we must do," I

continued. "We must not only be prepared for Chancel's attack, we must also have a counter of our own. Miss Smythe, please review our options."

And we spent the rest of the day thinking and rethinking and planning every possible contingency and outcome, until all of us were wholly exhausted.

Monday, December 20th

Shibe reported to me at noon. Chancel had made his expected offer through one of the surviving Vicepros, Geistzeit, and, per my instructions, he had accepted the challenge. We both felt that at least one other tender, possibly more, had already been presented to the uncommitted Sergeants, to provide a certain amount of insurance for Gartendrech.

At least we knew the name of another enemy. I decided at that point to dispense with all of the remaining Vicepros: they were just too damned dangerous.

"Prepare the charges," I ordered Shibe, and he saluted me and left.

I don't think either of us liked the other very much, but at least we had come to respect the other's abilities, and I suppose that's about all one can expect these days.

By mid-afternoon I had developed one of those tension headaches that just keep getting worse and worse, and Grace came in and began massaging my neck and upper back, and one thing led to another, and soon we were sprawled on the hideaway couch I had had installed the previous week, furiously going at it.

Things were just starting to look up when a deadpan voice drifted out of the 'puter:

So let us go then, you and I
To that dung heap in the sky....

"Shit!" I cried again. "Shitty shit shit."
And I lost it again.
"Double shit!"
I was furious.
The impersonal voice continued to drone on and on.
Grace just walked over to the thing and banged it on the top. The voice abruptly ceased.
"Oh, blessèd relief," I muttered.
Then she embraced me, and nuzzled my weary brow beneath the twin orbs of her warm breasts, and I felt like a child again, sad and lonely and lost at sea.
Drowning 'neath an ever-increasing pile of shit.
Trying to reach that bright red rose that was supposed to be planted just at the apex, only to find when I got there that it smelled like shit, too.
Where was I going?
What was I doing?
Why, Cy?

Dead fuckin' fly.

Tuesday, December 21st

The Inter-Fellian News Agency announced this morning that Dr. Theo Fell would be making a western

tour of the Fellian States of America during the following week, beginning at Seattle on Monday the 27th, and reaching Southern California on Thursday or Friday.

Just what I needed.

At the least, I would be expected to attend the meeting of the administrative leaders of the California Saints University System in Saugus. I had Grace put it on my schedule, and ordered the campus physical plant to begin a general sweep of the facilities, just in case.

Grace ordered lunch in, and asked me to join her. She arranged the food on a small conference table off to one side of the room.

"You have to eat," she pleaded.

My insides were in turmoil, and I didn't think food would help the situation, but I sat down anyway. I needed the company.

I took her left hand in mine.

"I just wanted to say, Grace," I offered, looking deep into her impenetrable eyes, "that if things go badly today, I deeply appreciate your help and support these past weeks. I couldn't have done this without you."

She blushed and dropped her gaze.

"If Chancel prevails," I continued, "I want you to switch sides immediately, and try to save yourself and your family. Please believe me when I tell you that I've always had your best interests at heart."

"I'll never forget what you did for me," Grace said, leaning over to kiss me.

Then we ate as much as we could stomach, just nibbles really, and talked about nothings at all.

The Faculty Senate convened promptly at one o'clock, with the usual obsequies and official pronunciamentos. All the players were present. I saw Chancel perched on his red throne down at the end of the table, and I nodded perfunctorily at him. He barely acknowledged my presence in return, although he smiled slightly. He anticipated much too much.

When it came my turn to make a report, I merely announced, "Move to adjourn," and everyone began yelling and banging on the table to catch Chair's attention.

"Point of order!" I screamed, and Chairman finally recognized me.

"A motion to adjourn," I stated, "is not subject to debate, and must be voted upon immediately."

"He's correct," said Parliamentarian Feuchtersleben, and the Chair just shrugged. What else could he do?

"All in favor," he ordered, and there was a roar of mingled voices.

Then, "All opposed," and another cacophony rose up to the rafters.

"Uh," he began, looking around at all of the expectant eyes, and finally down the table at my very cold ones, "uh, the ayes have it."

"Division!" screamed several of the Vicepros.

"A division has been requested," Chair stated. "All those in favor raise their hands."

Then, "All opposed."

Then, "Any abstentions?"

He turned to Parliamentarian.

Feuchtersleben finally finished his calculations.

"The ayes are fourteen, the nays fourteen, with two abstentions."

"The motion fails for lack of a majority," Chairman announced, and a great sigh filled the hall.

I just smiled to myself. Grace and Shibe had been carefully tabulating the votes, and now we knew on whom we could rely—and who had to go.

I signaled unobtrusively with my left hand, down below the level of the roundtable.

Captain Shibe marched forward with a sixsquad of his men, and demanded the floor.

"I hereby charge Vice Provost Geistzeit with treason against the University and with anti-Fellosophical thought," he intoned.

His cap was appropriately and neatly tucked beneath his left arm.

"Objection!" yelled Vicepro Hausensteiner.

"Vicepro?" acknowledged Chairman Churchyard.

"With all respect, as our dearly beloved Provost has already pointed out previously, Captain Shibe is head of the Saintpols," Hausensteiner stated, "and as such may not serve simultaneously as Sergeant-at-Arms of the Senate."

I raised my hand.

"Sergeant Shibe is serving only as Acting Captain of the Saintpols," I noted, "pending an official appointment to that position. His permanent post is Sergeant-at-Arms of the Faculty Senate."

"Then I move that Sergeant Shibe be confirmed in

his rank of Captain," Hausensteiner continued.

"I would not support such an advancement at this time," I indicated.

"Call for the question," the other shouted.

"Any further discussion?" Chair asked, looking about the room. "Hearing none, all those voting 'aye' please respond."

There was a roar of voices. The "nays" seemed equally balanced. When Chair ruled in my favor, a division was called.

"What is the final tally?" Chair inquired.

"Fourteen ayes, fourteen nays, and two abstentions," Parliamentarian stated.

"The motion fails for lack of a majority," Chair ruled.

Then I stood in my place, and pointed my finger directly at Hausensteiner.

"I accuse the Vicepro of attempting to subvert these proceedings," I stated, and ordered Shibe to arrest him.

Hausensteiner was a niggardly little man, dressed all in tweed and twaddling, and I was glad indeed to see his twitching ass hauled away kicking and screaming his *innocencia*.

He should have known, oh my brothers, oh yes indeed. No one is innocent in Fellian America.

Geistzeit was next, and then Vicepro Teufelspökel, and then Division Head Quenstedter, and so on. Within half an hour, I had removed eight members of the Senate, all real or potential opponents.

Then I moved that the Sergeant-at-Arms and the Chief Advocator of the California Saints University

both be granted permanent seats on the Senate, and the motion carried by an overwhelming majority. I also appointed acting heads for the newly vacant divisions from out of my own staff.

No one objected.

No one could.

Finally, I had my Chief Advocator deliver a sealed envelope to Chancel Gartendrech, who was beginning to squirm very uncomfortably indeed on his gilded throne. He opened it gingerly, pulled out an official paper, and then carefully examined the other contents (including some luscious photos!), but without showing them to anyone else. Finally he sighed, signed the document, gave it to Grace, and put the rest of the papers back in the envelope.

She brought the sheet back to me at the other end of the table.

I stood again.

"I regret to announce," I rumbled on in my most solemn voice, "that Chancel has resigned his position, effective immediately, due to reasons of health. I now assume the additional role of Acting Chancel of the University, pending confirmation of my position by the Board of Trustees of the California Saints University System. I know that all of you will be forthcoming with your assistance to help me through this very difficult time."

Murmurs of kudos and hidden grumbles emanated from around the table.

"Now let us praise Chancel Gartendrech for his

service to the campus community, and wish him well in his happy retirement."

I graciously led the applause as Shibe escorted him from the room. His days of leisure would be short indeed.

Then I stated, "I have come to the conclusion while watching these proceedings that the Faculty Senate squanders far too much of the valuable time of the campus administrators and faculty. I therefore propose to streamline its operations, in order to bring this august body more in tune with modern administrative requirements.

"First," I continued, "collegial relations between the faculty and administration can be preserved through a more limited schedule of regular meetings, to be held, say, once a term, and this I do propose.

"Second, I recognize the need of the faculty to be informed on an ongoing basis of those events which may have a bearing on the most efficient operation of their departments, and therefore I propose that the Executive Committee of the Senate perform these functions, meeting as needed throughout each term, and passing their information directly to those individuals who require that data.

"Third, I propose that the Faculty Senate Executive Committee shall consist in the future of the Chancel, the Provost, the Sergeant-at-Arms, and the Chief Advocator.

"I now request and require your active consideration of these measures, and I look forward to your accep-

tance of same."

I smiled very broadly. I was their friend. I was their mentor. I was their imperator.

And everyone knew it, too.

The vote was unanimously in favor. *Surprise! Surprise!*

I then moved to adjourn.

All in all, a most satisfactory day.

I celebrated by having dinner catered in the offices of the Provost for myself and the other members of our little triumvirate.

Wednesday, December 22nd

Shibe reported first thing in the morning that Chancel had hanged himself sometime during the night. I proposed that a marble monument in his honor be erected in the campus quad.

No one said nay, Ray.

Then I began systematically reorganizing the University administration so that the possibilities of dissent were greatly reduced. Video cameras were installed everywhere except in my offices. Grace was delegated the task of arranging the removal of the late Chancel's personal effects, and reported that we would be in our new quarters by Friday. I ordered that the Chancel Suite be expanded to encompass the offices on either side of it, which would become the official homes of Smythe and Shibe, my chief supporters.

Grace was ordered to filter all communications coming to me, so I won't be bothered with trivialities,

and Hamilcar to coordinate all of the new security measures being implemented.

We would have a smashingly good time!

I also made arrangements to occupy Chancel's hillside mansion by the weekend, and asked Grace to join me there on a permanent basis.

That afternoon, I was notified by the central office that the Board of Trustees, acting through *its* Executive Committee, had confirmed me in the rank of Chancellor of California Saints University.

Hoorah, hooray, it's another sunny day!

Thursday, December 23<u>rd</u>

Moving day, May.

Some of the furniture we junked, some we left untouched. I trust Grace's good taste in these matters. One thing I insisted upon was a more comfortable bed. I figured we'd need it!

I had a luncheon arranged with the one remaining Vicepro from the old administration, Porius Drachmann, a hoary old bastard who ran Physical Plant and Grounds, and who had already announced his retirement for next year. Several of the holdover division heads would also be joining us.

At noon Shibe and a sixsquad and I trotted over to Dragonetti Hall, site of the campus dining room. I had ordered some decent food prepared, instead of the usual dreck that was served at these things, and I was quite pleasantly surprised by the scrumptious repast that Celtisour managed to throw together in just one

day. It's amazing what a little firm guidance can do.

The surviving administrators displayed their total compliance in a number of different ways, including a proposal to rename Dragonetti Hall after *moi*, which I demurely accepted, after several protests. The ceremony would occur at the beginning of next term, on New Year's Day. We parted most amicably. I only spotted one of them who needed to be radicated right away.

As I was exiting the building, a Saintpol posted for guard duty suddenly pulled his weapon and began shooting at me, one of the bullets hitting close enough to my head that a chip of stone embedded itself in my right cheek.

Shibe's men immediately returned fire, and only had to kill two innocent studiants before bringing the man down.

I ordered his family wiped, just to make a point, and directed that his body be hung at the entrance to the campus for a month, for the crows to feast upon.

Back in my new office, my Grace gracefully restored my humor with some well-applied felicitations, and by bandaging my face. Thank Fell for her!

She would sing the savageness out of a bear,
She eases my savageness by being bare.

FYTTE THE NINTH

So let us go then, you and I
To that dung heap in the sky
Where the maggots play and
Flies buzz 'round and 'round,
Where administrators lost
And administrators found
Somehow find their way around,
And continue to expound
Upon the virtues of unsound
Management.

Friday, December 24th

Fell is coming, tra-la, tra-lay!

I got the news this morning. He's obviously heard of my lightning rise to the top, and wants to spend a few hours with me, a week from today. I can't believe it!

Grace and I just danced 'round and 'round the office, scarcely able to contain our joy.

This means great things for my career, I'm sure. Head Chancel of the entire Cal Saints System, encompassing some 163 campuses in Upper and Lower California, or perhaps, dare I suggest it, Head Chancel

of the Fellian States of America Collegial Education System? What I've done here could become a model for the entire country.

> *You told me a lie, an odious damned lie;*
> *Upon my soul, a lie, a wicked lie,*
> *Oh my, says I, dead fuckin' fly!*

Monday, December 27th

The three of us spent the weekend in our offices, directing a massive effort by our employees to clean and repaint and replant the University, to make it more presentable to our glorious leader.

Only one glitch marred the preparations. I was directing the placement of a banner welcoming Chairman Fell, when a piece of concrete fell without warning from the side of the library building, striking and instantly killing the worker standing next to me. I was splattered with his blood and brains, and had to change for lunch. I don't recall the man's name.

After the meal, Shibe brought me something he'd retrieved from the scene.

"We found this pasted on the fifth floor balcony," he stated, "where a piece of the structure had been deliberately worked loose."

He handed me a flyer, torn where it had been wrenched free. It was the scarlet image of fly lying on its back, its legs waving idly in the air. The illustration was signed "*D.F.*"

I blanched. This was beginning to get serious.

"The attack was deliberate?" I asked.

"It can't be anything else, sir," he responded. "We'll increase security, of course, but I would strongly recommend that you limit your outside appearances for a while."

"I can't," I protested, "not with Chairman Fell coming on Friday. We must appear to be conducting business as usual."

"Well," he said, "we'll have to increase security anyway with the Great Leader parading around campus, so we have every excuse to beef up your detail as well, and to post marksmen here and there on top of the buildings—and also to prevent access to such things as external balconies."

"Make it so," I ordered.

I wasn't happy about the situation, but all I had to do was get through this week without a national incident, and my reputation was secured.

The social decisions, the dinners, the presentations and such, I left completely in Grace's capable hands. After all, she knew how to use them so well.

> *The more angel she, Sheree,*
> *And you the blacker devil, Neville.*

Tuesday, December 28th

Since Fell will be here on Friday, I have decided not to attend the meeting of the Chancels of the CSUS in Saugus on Thursday. There's simply no point in risking a public appearance with so much at stake.

Shibe and Smythe both agree with me.

As for the rest of the campus, everyone seems excited about the good Doctor's impending visit. I've ordered an unprecedented level of security, and I've already decided to maintain it once he's gone.

In the meantime, I finally moved into the late Chancel's residence today. I wanted to give the workers time to remodel the place, since Dr. F. will be staying there as my guest for at least one evening, possibly even for the weekend. He may actually make his New Year's Day address from my home!

What can I say, Fay? All things come to those who wait.

Shibe is still concerned over several minor security lapses, however, and the impossibility of checking the bona fides of all of the new personnel we've added to the squads. Another copy of the D.F. poster has appeared, tacked to a restroom stall in the Pflanzerbaltin Administration Building. This time the fly, still on its back, is being flushed down the toilet.

Shibe asked what it meant, and I responded that I didn't know. He indicated the difficulty of tracing the perps without additional contextual information, which, of course, I can never ever give him.

Why do my triumphs always seem to be shadowed by the dark side of the farce?

Wednesday, December 29th

Fell is touring Frisco today, where it's pouring down sheets of rain on his entourage. I saw the little man

being escorted into Aurangzeb Hall, but he didn't look at all pleased with the arrangements. I ordered Grace to view the tape, and she made appropriate notes on things not to do here.

I've had no time recently to pursue our relationship, and strangely, I don't miss it much. I wonder why.

Two more days, just two more days.

Later

Shibe just brought me another copy of that damned poster. This one shows a second fly, apparently eating the corpus of the first.

How utterly disgusting.

How utterly depraved!

Thursday, December 30th

We're frantically continuing our efforts to spruce up the campus, but I think we're almost there. More variants of the fly flyer, each viler, Tyler, than the last, have magically appeared, but there's nothing I can do or say that will make them go away.

Köhlflauer, my contact among the Trustees, just phoned me with an account of Dr. Fell's meeting with the System heads. The CSUS was heavily criticized for its lack of initiative and failure to conform to national Fellian standards, all except for our University. I was singled out by name as a positive example for the rest.

Woo hoo, Lou!

I'm as ready as I'll ever be.

I'm as horny as a manatee.

Friday, December 31<u>st</u>

The great day arrived clear and warm, one of those glorious midwinter days that Southern California can occasionally offer the weary traveler. A light Santa Ana stirred our hair and formal clothes as the helicopter containing Dr. Fell approached from the West.

Finally, the craft touched down on the open campus quad, and discharged our Glorious Leader and his entourage. He was shorter than I expected, and older, with wispy gray hair and a gray suit that looked as if it had come right out of the history books. Everything about him sang out, "This is a great man."

Greater than I, Hy.

We formed a reception line, with me in the lead, and Dr. Fell touched each of us in turn as he passed. His hand was cool and firm, and he looked me right in the eye before saying, "I commend you, good Chancel, for all your work on our behalf."

Then I followed him down the ranks to introduce him to the members of my administration, one by one, and he graciously offered them his good will and thanks. When he was finished, we proceeded to a formal luncheon at Dragonetti Hall, where several toasts were made back and forth, the final one being a round of drinks in my honor.

I couldn't have been more pleased had I planned it this way.

Afterwards, he joined me and my two comrades in

the conference room off my new office suite.

"I must say," he commented, looking around at the newly-painted walls and well-kept facilities, "you have done an extraordinary job with this place. You are obviously intended for great things, Chancel. I was wondering if you might consider a national position with me sometime in the very near future."

"Of course," I responded. "Whatever did you have in mind?"

"I was thinking of creating a national system of higher education by uniting all of the state universities into one unit."

He lifted up a dainty right hand, and carefully examined the manicured nails for flaws.

"Naturally, I would need someone I could trust to weave together the disparate threads of regionalism into one strong rope that can be used to strangle all creativity and original thought. If you see what I mean."

"Perfectly," I commented. "And I assure you that I'm your man, Fran."

"Of course, I had thought when I first took office," he continued, "to allow as many of our traditional institutions as possible to survive intact, but I can see now that this was an unfortunate mistake, Jake. It is perfectly apparent to me, as it is to every member of my central administration, that nothing must fly in the face of the ointment."

"What?" I said.

I had missed something in that last sentence.

"You!" he stated, pointing his right index finger right

at me, "*you* will become the instrument of change. And if you fail, fella, there's always another, brother."

"Dead fly," says I.

He looked at me curiously, his head cocked to one side, and smiled his crooked smile, flashing a gold tooth.

"So they say, Ray," he replied.

He looked again around my office, and then asked me a curious question.

"How did you manage to keep hidden, Edwin?" he wanted to know.

"My predecessor, when it appeared that he was about to fall, Paul," I related, "lent me his fears, gave me his tears."

"You speak of Latepro Bork?" he asked. "The dork?"

"None other," says I. "He assisted me with strategies, with passwords to the U-net, and with this"—I pulled the little silencer out of my pocket, twirling it in my hand so the light flashed off its sides.

"What is it?" he inquired.

"It dampens the sound so that it can't be recorded," I responded.

"Indeed," he commented. "Chancel, I am unaware of the existence of such a device, or at least of anything that would be effective against our top-rated audio equipment, and surely I would know."

"Then what...."

The room suddenly became very quiet.

"Toss it here," he ordered.

I lofted it underhanded across the table, and he

caught the thing with his small right hand. A flash of light nearly blinded me, and as I slowly regained my sight, I saw him slumped down in the chair opposite, clutching his unmoving chest.

Grace was holding a small mirror under his nose, and she shook her head. Then she used a pencil to snag the device through an opening in its side, and carefully put it into a plastic bag. She handed it to Shibe.

"Call the Emergency Medical Services!" I commanded.

She just looked at me and smiled. So sweet.

"I don't think that they can help our Glorious Leader right now," she said. "His heart has failed, or so it will appear *post mortem*."

Then she came over to my chair and unexpectedly jabbed my chest with a Taser, leaving me temporarily paralyzed.

"I'm truly sorry, Chancel," she said, "but I can't have you interfering just now. Hamilcar and I need time to tidy things up before we disappear into the underground, so to speak. We've accomplished what we set out to do, and you've been very helpful in that regard. I doubt the authorities will believe what you tell them, and I'm quite sure they will take extraordinary efforts to discover the real 'truth.' You should find this time a unique experience, one particularly suited to your character."

She bent over and kissed me on the cheek.

"One for the road, eh?" she laughed.

"Come on, Grace," Shibe urged, putting an arm

around her waist.

He reached over and pinched my nose.

"Don't believe everything you read, Bede," he stated, smiling.

Then they left, carefully securing the door behind them, and I was left to my own thoughts.

The charge wore off in half an hour, but by then it was too late to call security. No one would believe that I waited that long without some ulterior motive being involved.

So instead, I went over to the 'puter, turned it on, watched the message, "*Dead Fly*" flash in all its ruddy glory, and set about completing this record for posterity.

I had just finished when they began pounding on my door. I made no effort to respond. They would get inside soon enough, Duff. I just reached over and turned off the machine.

Just like this, Chris:

> *As for me, I*
> *Have nothing left to cry*
> *Save these few words,*
> *Dead Fly, Dead Fly.*

EPILOGUE

Saturday, February 11th

He stepped back from the console, watching it fade to black, and took a seat at the conference table.

"I'm sorry to have put you through this ordeal," Provost said, "but I wanted you to see this for yourselves."

He glanced around the room, letting his eyes rest successively on Chancel Gartendrech, the five Vicepros, Captain Tannenbaum, Sergeant Wickhizer, Saintpol Shibe, and Advocator Smythe, who was sitting in the corner, head buried in her hands, quietly sobbing.

"How was this uncovered?" Geistzeit wanted to know.

Bork sighed. "Several days after Parrott's execution, one of the technicians in the Property Room was gathering together his things for shipment to his widow, and noticed that the heel on one shoe was loose. Inside he found a minidisk containing this file. The wife knew nothing about it. She's already been radicated."

"Why, he must have been insane," Chancel noted. "Just for the record, who occupied the cubicle next to

his?"

"Someone named Burgess," Provost indicated. "He was taken in September, right after school started. The psychpols think that this incident was what set Parrott off."

"And who was this Burgess?" Gartendrech pressed.

"A nobody," Bork replied, "a librarian. He'd been with the campus for forty years, and never made any impression. I hadn't even heard of him until this happened."

"Of what was he accused?"

"Oh, just the usual," Provost continued. "We received an anonymous tip about his anti-Fellticanism, and arrested him. He confessed to everything in the end."

"Don't they all," Chancel commented. "And you're sure, Harminius, that's all there is to this? He wasn't a member of the Underground?"

"Absolutely not," Bork stated.

"Very well. You'll see to it, of course."

Then Gartendrech looked at each of them in turn with his cold black eyes.

"None of you have ever heard this, or considered it, or even thought of it. None of you will repeat any anything you've seen. Understood?"

Then the Chancellor wrapped himself in his scarlet cloak and left the room, the others following closely in his train, save only for Provost and his Advocator.

When the door was firmly closed, Grace finally looked up, her eyes red, her cheeks stained with tears.

"*How* could he know?" she gasped. "How *could* he, Harmin? How could he say such things?"

Bork rushed over to her and gathered her in his arms.

"I don't know, dearest," he said. "I really don't know. We live in very strange times. But we'll survive. We always have. And one day...."

"One day what?" she responded. "Do you *really* think they'll ever stop? I don't. I believe that poor madman knew exactly what he was talking about. I don't see *any* future, Harmin, for us or for them. One day they'll get us. That's as certain as certain can be. One day soon we'll be discovered, and then it's the ovens for us."

"So what's it to be then, eh?" Bork questioned. "I certainly won't risk your life."

"Our lives are already demarcated by crosshatches," she shouted. "X's and O's in rapid succession, and then the straight line right through the middle. You know I'm right. Unless we take that risk, we have no future, together or separately."

"Then we know what we have to do," he agreed. "Parrott has laid it all out for us, right there on that disk. We set them feeding upon each other, and let them do the business themselves. Let the blood flow freely. Then we step in and take over."

"You realize," she said, "that once we start down this road, there's no going back."

"In truth," he smiled back at her, ruffling her hair slightly, "there never was, I think. But I'm basically an optimist, Grace. Whether we succeed or whether

we fail, others will come after us. A year from now, a hundred years, a thousand, maybe, the Dr. Fells of this world will fall before the combined will of the people. Somehow, somewhere, someone will shout 'Enough!'—and the tyrants will tremble in their pretty mansions of overblown philosophies. Maybe poor demented Parrott, wherever he is, will wake at that point, and take the only satisfaction that he can."

"Then let's make a promise to ourselves, Harmin," she stated, kissing him gently. "Let's be kind to each other, enjoy each day to the fullest, and try to live, while still we can."

She kissed him again, this time hard, and stopped only for a breath.

"Now that's a bargain I will gladly keep, Veep," he said, and suddenly there was no more time for words.

He idly swatted away a fly that had landed on her shoulder, and it spiraled down to the carpet, coming to rest on its back, its dead, twitching legs reaching futilely into the air.

AFTERWORD
"DEAD FLY"

It started with a single line:

"They came for Barrett this morning."

My friend and colleague Buckley Barrett occupied the office next to mine in the basement of the concrete tomb where we worked and played, with Beverly Ryan planted on the opposite side. Just to the right of his door was the stairwell to the first floor, which, back in those halycon days of good health, I could ascend two steps at a time, running full-tilt. It led directly to the administrative offices.

That *our* personal offices existed at all was due to a variety of factors, including the institution of union bargaining in the CSU in the early 1980s, and my willingness to fight for what I perceived to be the basic rights of myself and my fellow faculty. I filed a series of grievances that forced the administration to grant us sabbatical leaves, and to build us more-or-less private offices with such modern amenities as telephones (!) and desks and chairs—and doors that could be locked.

This did not make me popular with the powers-that-

were back in those days. Indeed, I wondered at times how long I'd be able to stand the constant pressure and petty harassment to which I was periodically subjected; and without the support of my long-suffering wife, Mary, I suspect that I wouldn't have lasted very long. But, in the end, *I* was the one who lasted forty years, outliving everyone who'd been there when I started in September of 1970.

There's no particular virtue in longevity. I learned to reinvent myself, personally and professionally, over and over again; and when I became stymied or bored or just angry at the stupidities of certain members of the academy, I turned to my writing to find a temporary surcease to my frustration and pain. That didn't end or cure my paranoia, but it did help (it still does).

Academentia was one of my answers, but initially, I found myself unable to get past the first page or two. That section was probably written sometime in the early 1990s (I didn't date the composition of my fiction back then). I penned the first few paragraphs, *sans* the verse, and just didn't know where to go with it. I was too close to the material. *I* was the anonymous narrator, if anyone was, and the agony that I felt was very real to me, if to no one else save Mary.

A few years later I was finally given something *real* to do, something commensurate with my talents, and that enabled me to gain some distance from the material (eventually). Also, in 1995 I wrote a bit of doggerel for my boss's fiftieth birthday celebration, which was chanted by a chorus of my staff for the occasion; it

was a takeoff on T. S. Eliot's "The Love Song of J. Alfred Prufrock," Sean Kelly's *National Lampoon* parody, "The Love Song of J. Edgar Hoover," and Don Marquis's "Archy and Mehitabel" series.

And then I suddenly realized, in 1999, that the two pieces actually could be merged together in some terribly absurd way, and once I had that idea, I was able to complete the novel very quickly in November of that year. The verse ("Dead Fly") was reworked to fit the needs of the story.

I also changed Buckley's name to Parrott, since I didn't want the character I'd created to have any association with my dear friend (they're nothing alike); and I invented Dr. Theo Fell and the fascist religious regime that he imposed upon America—which seems to me an even greater possibility these days than a dozen years ago.

And the result was...well, I don't know. It's both like and unlike anything else I ever did or have done to date. I adopted a sing-song, repetitive pattern of language that might be unique to the narrator—or perhaps just reflect the culture at the time. The storyteller's ongoing deterioration, either from a mental ailment or from the stress generated by his attempts to survive, leave the reader in a quandary about what to believe, about what's real (in the context of the tale), and what isn't. I deliberately maintained an almost surreal backdrop to the narrative, which is emphasized by the verses that underly each section—including the ongoing saga of "Dead Fly." And what does "Dead Fly" really mean,

anyway?

As with some of my other fictions, there are no clear answers to these questions, either for the narrator or for us. Is he mad (angry) or mad (insane)? I don't honestly know—perhaps a bit of both.

But for me, *Academentia* proved to be a transition piece, from *The Dark-Haired Man*, my first long novel, which was told in the third person, to my later works. *This* was the tale that featured my first extended story told solely from the point-of-view of the main character, a conceit that allows the writer the potential of having the narrator lie both to himself and to the reader. And I think it still works, in some curious fashion or another.

This work was initially published in my first story collection, *Katydid & Other Critters*, which made no impression at all when it first appeared. I decided to resurrect it for the Wildside Doubles series, and was pleased when my friend, W. C. Bamberger, agreed to have it featured with his own compelling work.

I hope you agree that it was worth disinterment.

Blessèd be:

Robert Reginald
18 March 2011

ABOUT THE AUTHOR

ROBERT REGINALD was born in Japan, and lived in Turkey as a youth. He starting writing as a child, and penned his first book during his senior year in college. He settled in Southern California in 1969, where he served as an academic librarian for forty years. He now edits the Borgo Press imprint of Wildside Press, and has also penned more than 120 books and 13,000 short pieces.

He loves to hear from his readers. You can find him at:

www.millefleurs.tv